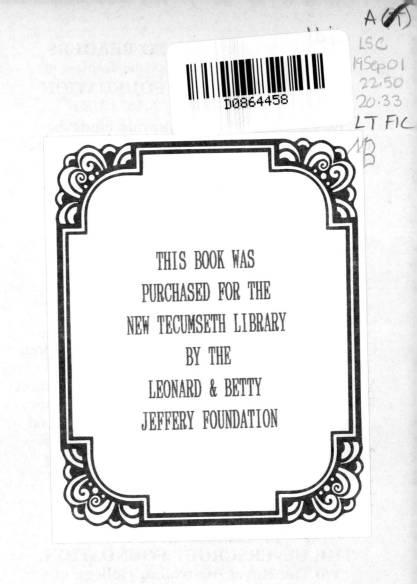

THE GREAT ADVENTURE

When Charlotte went to Cornwall to stay with her cousins, she hoped that at last she would achieve her ambition — to have an adventure. To her disappointment, she found that life there was just as dull as it was at home. But when she persuaded her cousin to dress in men's clothes in order to escape from the house and go to the fair, Charlotte was soon embarked on a far greater and more dangerous adventure than she had ever dreamed of.

Books by Charlotte Grey
in the Linford Romance Library:

GOLDEN BUTTERFLY
SUMMER IN HANOVER SQUARE

CHARLOTTE GREY

THE GREAT ADVENTURE

Complete and Unabridged

LINFORD
Leicester

First published in Great Britain in 1983 by
Robert Hale Limited
London

First Linford Edition
published 2001
by arrangement with
Robert Hale Limited
London

British Library CIP Data

Grey, Charlotte
    The great adventure.—Large print ed.—
    Linford romance library
    1. Love stories
    2. Large type books
    I. Title
    823.9′14 [F]

    ISBN 0–7089–4572–4

Published by
F. A. Thorpe (Publishing)
Anstey, Leicestershire

Set by Words & Graphics Ltd.
Anstey, Leicestershire
Printed and bound in Great Britain by
T. J. International Ltd., Padstow, Cornwall

This book is printed on acid-free paper

1

'Oh, Charlotte, we should never have come!' Kitty's teeth chattered like castanets as she whispered hoarsely to her cousin. 'Positively, we should never have come!'

'Be quiet!' Charlotte hissed back. 'Or they'll hear us!'

And she pulled her cousin farther back into the shadow of the huge rock.

Both girls stared appalled at the scene before them. They were a few hundred yards from the top of the cliffs above Melyn Cove. A half-moon was standing high in the sky, large enough to give out sufficient light which now came glittering down on a procession of men and heavily-laden donkeys, which were toiling in single file up from the beach below. The leading man and the donkey were nearly level with the girls; the last in the line had only just left the

1

beach. Tensely the girls watched as the first smuggler walked very near them, Charlotte holding Kitty by the arm, both girls holding their breaths.

It was a malign fate which caused Kitty to be assailed by a tickle in her nose at the very moment the smuggler drew level with them. Desperately the girl attempted to control her sneeze, but it was far too powerful for her. The silence of the night, hitherto broken only by the plodding footfalls of the trudging donkeys, was suddenly rent by a sneeze of what seemed to the cowering girls to be of gargantuan proportions.

'Who's there?' the man demanded in a low voice, stopping and looking towards them. The terrified girls saw the moonlight glint on the blade of the knife he drew. He left his donkey, which stood patiently, and advanced towards the shadow of the rock. At once he saw the two girls, and made a grab to seize them. Petrified, Charlotte and Kitty allowed him to drag them

2

forward out of the shadow.

'Hah! Two young gennelmen, I see!' the smuggler said, looking them up and down.

For so the girls appeared. Both were dressed in men's clothes, and their unpowdered hair was tied back severely with black ribbons.

'An' what might 'ee be a-doin' of 'ere at this time o' night?' the smuggler demanded threateningly in a low voice.

'We — we — we are returning from the — f — fair — at Trevannock!' Charlotte got out, recovering herself first.

'Gennelmen — *walking*!' the smuggler jeered.

'Our — our horses went lame. We had to leave them in the inn in Trevannock,' Charlotte returned, improvising now.

'Well now, there's a thing! And where might 'ee be walking?'

'To — to St. Bride's.'

The second smuggler and his donkey now moved over to them. The first one said, "'Ere's two young gennelmen walking 'ome in the moonlight, Jake,' he said in a derisory voice. 'What do 'ee think us should do wi' they?'

'Tip 'em o'er the cliff,' the second man returned without hesitation.

'Oh, no!' Kitty squealed. Then, remembering her attire: 'Oh, no!' she repeated in a slightly deeper voice.

'Bain't no 'arm done, Jake,' the first man said easily, grinning at the two girls. 'I say us takes they wi' us.'

Another squeak issued from Kitty.

The first man turned to her. 'You'd rather go o'er the cliff, me luvver?' he asked good-humouredly.

'No! Oh, no!'

'Then you'll come along o' us, me beauties!'

And with that the man proceeded to untie the scarf round his neck. His companion grunted, then did likewise, and the first man went on, 'Now, if you gennelmen'll promise to keep as quiet as mice, and not cry out or try to escape, we'll do nought but blindfold 'ee. Don' 'ee worry; us'll let 'ee go later. Now; do 'ee promise?'

'Oh, yes!' both girls whispered in chorus, and the smugglers proceeded to tie the rags over their eyes.

Now the girls could see nothing, but they heard the footsteps of more men and beasts near them.

To their surprise, they heard a cultured voice demanding, 'What's up, Tregarth?'

'Two young gennelmen who've seen more'n them ought, that's all, sir. Them'll come along o' us for a while, an' then us'll loose they.'

'I see.'

The same voice then spoke swiftly in French and was answered in the same tongue.

It was only a few moments before the procession was on its way again, headed by the man called Tregarth, who was holding Charlotte by one arm, and behind came Jake, grasping Kitty equally firmly. There was no opportunity for the girls to give each other

5

courage by walking beside each other. They had to advance unhelped into the unknown, stumbling over the uneven ground, terrified as to the outcome of their journey, dependent entirely upon the goodwill of their captors.

They had plenty of time to consider their predicament. Truth to tell, it was largely Charlotte's fault, as she now most ruefully admitted to herself. Charlotte Radley had recently come to stay with her Cornish cousins for a long holiday, hoping for and expecting excitement. Her uncle, Jonathan Radley, was the vicar of St. Bride's, and having been widowed long years ago, his household had been run ever since by his sister, Miss Radley, a spinster of commanding mien, who believed that young ladies, even of eighteen, should on the whole be seen and not heard. And far from any adventures such as Charlotte had hoped for, there had been no schemes, and only dreary card-parties.

When Charlotte, who was just

eighteen, had proposed that she and Kitty should go to the fair at Trevannock, their aunt Radley had forbidden it in scandalised tones, saying that it was not fit for gentlefolk, being full of rogues and vagabonds and thieves, and other such villains.

Charlotte, an only child, and accustomed to having pretty much her own way with her easy-going parents at home in Shropshire, had not been at all pleased at this prohibition. She had been dismayed to find that life with her cousins down in the Lizard peninsula was excessively dull, the aforesaid card-parties, and calling upon her aunt's elderly cronies, not being at all to her taste. The local spring fair, therefore, possessed greater attraction than it might otherwise have done, and Charlotte determined to go, in spite of her aunt Radley; and it had not taken her long to persuade her amenable cousin Kitty that they should go secretly.

In the circumstances it was quite out of the question to take a maid with them, and so Charlotte had daringly suggested that they should go dressed in men's clothes, and, without leave, they had borrowed garments for their purpose from Kitty's brother Tom. And after telling their aunt that they were going to spend the day with Kitty's friend, Amelia Bourden, the two had slipped out, and had walked the four miles to Trevannock early in the morning, and had spent a lively day there. They had enjoyed themselves so much that they had set out for home later than they had intended, and had been overtaken by the dark and the smugglers while they had still one more mile to traverse.

Now as they blundered along, both girls would have given a good deal to be safe back at the St. Bride's vicarage, and would most cheerfully have endured a scold from their aunt Radley.

How long they walked blindfolded, neither had the least idea, but after what seemed hours, they were ordered to stop. They heard the burdened donkeys move past them, while Tregarth remained with the girls. Gradually the sound of the animals' hoofbeats died away, and Charlotte plucked up courage to address their captor.

'W — what are you going to do with us now?' she asked in a voice which quavered somewhat in spite of all her efforts.

There was no reply, and Charlotte spoke again.

When there was still no answer, she whispered tentatively, 'Kitty?'

'Yes?' came the whispered reply.

'Have they gone?'

'It seems so . . .'

Charlotte at once put her hands to her head and tore off the blindfold. She blinked a little at first, then as her eyes grew accustomed to the light which was now much dimmer than it had been near the sea, she saw that they were alone on an earth track which disappeared into the distance to their right. On the left it proceeded for a short way before turning a corner, and became lost behind a small copse. Fields lay on either side.

'Kitty! We're quite alone!' Charlotte cried. 'Here, let me help you.' And she proceeded to pull off her cousin's blindfold. 'Do you know where we are?' she demanded anxiously.

Kitty looked up and down the road. 'No — o,' she said slowly. 'Oh, Charlotte, what shall we do now?'

'Well, let us walk this way,' Charlotte said practically, indicating the way to the left. 'You might recognise some-thing past the trees.'

They did as Charlotte suggested, both peering anxiously about them. At first neither girl recognised anything, but after about ten minutes they came to a cross-roads, where stood a gibbet on which hung the skeleton of a dead malefactor. There was no wind to rattle the bones, but the sight was gruesome enough in the dim light, and the girls gripped each other's hands tightly, and hurried past at a run, neither speaking

10

till the grisly object was well behind them.

'Well,' panted Charlotte, 'do you recognise anything yet, Kitty?'

The other girl nodded, and swallowed once or twice before she was able to speak. 'I-I think that was the gibbet at Polteath Cross. If it is, we are only about half a mile from St. Bride's.'

'Oh, thank heaven for that!' Charlotte exclaimed gratefully.

And the two went forward with renewed energy.

A few minutes later they could make out the tower of St. Bride's church, and a little more than ten minutes later they were standing outside the vicarage gate.

It was clear that all was not as it should be within. There were lights at several of the windows, and the sound of voices calling loud enough to be heard. The girls looked at each other.

'What are we going to do?' Kitty whispered.

'There's nothing for it. We will have to go in!' Charlotte said determinedly.

'Aunt Radley will be very cross,' Kitty said fearfully.

'Well, I shall tell her that it was all my fault — that I persuaded you,' Charlotte returned decidedly. 'After all, it is quite true. You would never have gone to the fair but for me. I really am very sorry, Kitty, that I should have dragged you into such a scrape.'

'It is not all your fault at all, Charlotte!' Kitty said bravely. 'I need not have gone with you if I had not wished.'

'No. But nor would you have thought of going had it not been for me.' Charlotte straightened herself. 'Come on, Kitty!'

'But — Charlotte — we can not go like this!' And Kitty gestured at the male garments they were wearing. 'Aunt Radley would have a convulsion.'

That made Charlotte pause. Certainly her aunt would consider the wearing of men's clothes an even more heinous crime than disobedience. 'Well, we must get in without being seen, then.'

'But how?'

'We must climb up the ivy outside our window!'

'But we could never do it!'

'What else do you suggest?'

Kitty was silent, but followed Charlotte as she crept cautiously round the vicarage wall, then through the garden gate and across the lawn till they were at the side of the building under their own window. Without pause, Charlotte began to climb up the creeper, inching upwards carefully, and making as little noise as she could.

'Supposing the window is closed, Charlotte?' Kitty whispered anxiously.

'Then I shall have to open it!' Charlotte returned, continuing to climb.

Luckily the vicarage was an old building constructed in Tudor times, and so was not very high. Kitty watched as her cousin went upwards, and when

Charlotte reached the recently-installed sash-window, she found that it was open about four inches at the bottom, and hissed down, 'It's open, Kitty.'

Very carefully she tried to ease it upwards with one hand while clinging to the ivy with the other. Thanks to her aunt's impeccable housekeeping, the window slid upwards smoothly, and Charlotte managed to haul herself over the sill.

She had just got her feet to the floor when a young voice close beside her said, 'Boo!'

Charlotte let out a muffled shriek, and a girl's voice giggled.

'Anne! How could you!' Charlotte exclaimed, cross through fright.

Kitty's younger sister demanded, 'Charlotte! Where have you been! Aunt Radley is in such a taking!'

Charlotte glared at Anne, then turned back to the window. Her cousin was nearly level with the sill.

'Help me get Kitty in, Anne!' Charlotte commanded; and together they hauled the other girl into the room.

'Thank you!' Kitty gasped, leaning against the window and panting.

'Well, where *have* you been?' Anne demanded again. 'And what on earth are you wearing! Oh, you will be in such trouble! Lady Bourden and Amelia have been here and said that they had seen nothing of you, and our aunt was exceedingly cross, and Papa sent Tom and Peter to search the orchard and the church, and Aunt Radley has looked everywhere herself from the attics to the cellars, and is now sure that you are both drowned in the duck pond!'

'Oh, Charlotte!' Kitty cried, dismayed.

'Don't be foolish, Anne,' Charlotte said uncomfortably.

But her fifteen-year-old cousin shook her head. 'It is true! Aunt is talking of dragging it in the morning!'

'Oh, Charlotte! What are we going to do?' Kitty cried.

'Well the first thing,' Charlotte said practically, 'is to get out of these clothes. When we have our own clothes on, we will be in a far better state to face Aunt Radley.'

'But where have you *been*?' Anne demanded again.

'Nowhere that concerns you,' Charlotte returned loftily.

'If you don't tell me, I will go straight to Aunt Radley!' Anne threatened.

'Anne! You wouldn't!' Kitty cried.

'Tell me where you have been, then.'

Charlotte and Kitty were now taking off Tom's garments.

'We went to Trevannock fair,' Charlotte said, tugging the shirt over her head.

'You didn't!' Anne exclaimed, staring at her cousin with round eyes. 'Aunt said that — '

'It's quite true, Anne,' Kitty said. 'And you must promise not to say a word, mind!'

'Who did you go with?' Anne

returned. 'Did our cousin, Bob Prit-chard, take you?'

'Certainly not!' Kitty returned, going rosy red. 'We went alone.'

'Oh, what was it like? What did you do? I wish *I* had gone. Did you have your fortunes told?' Anne demanded.

'It was the greatest fun. We saw the fattest lady in the world, and a sheep with two heads, and we watched a play, and some tumblers, and yes, we had our fortunes told,' Charlotte laughed, good-humoured again, and pulling on her own gown.

'What did the gypsy say?'

'Oh, Kitty is to marry a local boy with brown hair and blue eyes,' Charlotte teased, describing Bob Prit-chard. 'And I am to be blessed with a tall, dark and handsome stranger.'

Kitty looked as though she was about to speak at that, but she said nothing, and continued to put on her own dress. In a few minutes both girls were once again arrayed as became young ladies.

'Do we — do we *have* to meet Aunt tonight?' Kitty whispered.

'Of course we do!' Charlotte answered more bravely than she felt. 'We can not let her think that we are drowned in the duck pond!'

Attempting to appear confident because of Anne, and to encourage themselves, the two girls ventured into the passage and made their way along it to the head of the staircase, closely followed by Anne, anxious not to miss any of the expected fireworks.

Slowly the girls descended the staircase, aware of a bustle and the sound of voices below. They were but halfway down the stairs when the door of the vicar's study burst open, and Tom Radley came out. At once he saw the girls on the staircase.

'Here they are!' he exclaimed loudly. 'Father! Aunt! They are here!'

The vicar and Miss Radley hurried into the hall, followed by the vicar's younger sons, Jack and Henry. Two footmen and the cook emerged from the door to the offices.

As all these eyes turned upwards to look at them, the girls froze where they were, staring down with a half-fearful, half-defiant gaze.

It was Aunt Bradley who recovered herself first. 'Where have you been?' she demanded in a thundering tone. 'Charlotte, Catherine, *where have you been*? We have all been exceedingly worried. Catherine, your father was about to call the constable.'

'I — I am very sorry, ma'am,' Kitty began in a small voice, trembling very much.

'Well?' Miss Radley continued in the same terrible tone; 'Where have you two been?'

'We — we — we went out, ma'am — ' Kitty blurted out, then stopped, quite unable to utter more.

'So I collect,' her aunt almost hissed in return. 'To Lady Bourden's, no doubt?' And Miss Radley glared up at her.

'N — no, ma'am,' Charlotte said

hesitatingly. 'We — we went for a walk instead.'

'Indeed!' Miss Radley's tone was sufficient to make a strong man quail. 'From early this morning — until now?'

'Yes, ma'am.' Charlotte had now recovered herself somewhat, and spoke with more confidence. 'And we meant to be returned a great deal earlier, ma'am, but — we have had the most dreadful, most terrifying experience!' The girl came a few steps further down the staircase and addressed her uncle. 'We were abducted, sir!' she proclaimed indignantly, her bosom heaving with outrage.

'Abducted!' The vicar blinked uncertainly.

'Yes, sir! By villains — smugglers, sir!'

'Smugglers!' The vicar and his three sons burst out in varying degrees of astonishment and excitement.

'And — where did this — abduction — take place, pray?' Miss Radley demanded in a voice acid with disbelief.

'We were walking along the cliff top to Melyn Cove, ma'am; but when we arrived, we found a train of donkeys coming up the cliff. They were laden with barrels — brandy, I suppose. We — we tried to hide, but the wretches discovered us, and tied us up, and made us go with them. And we have been in this condition — for hours! Indeed, we thought our last hour had come, ma'am, but fortunately they let us go somewhere near Polteath Cross, which luckily Kitty recognised, for all it was now dark, and we hurried home as fast as we could!'

And Charlotte looked from her uncle to her aunt, the picture of injured innocence. Kitty stared at her cousin's back in astonishment, while Anne smothered a giggle.

'Oh, what were they like? Tell us what they were like!' Jack and Henry cried.

'Be quiet, boys!' Miss Radley commanded. She returned her attention to her errant nieces. 'Then why did you not come to us immediately with this tale? Why did you first go to your room?' she demanded suspiciously.

'We were considerably dishevelled, ma'am,' Charlotte answered smoothly. 'In fact, we felt certain that we looked so unkempt that had you seen us in that state, you might have feared . . . in short,' Charlotte ended, her invention failing her momentarily, ' — in short, we feared to alarm you unduly, ma'am, and thought it best to tidy ourselves before coming to you.'

'Well, I am very relieved to see you both, my dears,' the vicar said mildly; 'very thankful indeed.'

'We are very thankful to be home safely, sir,' Charlotte said sincerely, coming down the remainder of the stairs and kissing her uncle on the cheek. 'And really, I was shocked to see so many smugglers abroad,' she went on virtuously. 'I can not think what the revenue men are doing to leave so many miscreants at large. My father is always complaining that we pay taxes enough, and yet these villains seem to come and go as they wish.'

'I had better go to the constable at once, had I not, sir?' Tom said.

'Oh, no — I daresay it will be far too late to catch any of them now,' the vicar said. 'Best leave it, my boy. We can decide what to do in the morning.'

'We heard the names of two of the men, sir,' Charlotte put in. 'The one who seized me was called Tregarth. That should be some help, sir, should not it?'

'Oh — er — yes, I dare say it might,' the vicar said, sounding even vaguer than usual. 'Though, you know, my dear, there are a good many Tregarths in this part of Cornwall.'

Miss Radley continued to be very suspicious, but the vicar suggested that some wine might not come amiss, and her mind was distracted when Charlotte remarked that she was exceedingly hungry, and at once she ordered a cold collation to be brought for her two nieces. Thankfully, then,

Charlotte and Kitty realised that they were to avoid a scolding.

★ ★ ★

Later that night, when Charlotte and Kitty were in bed in the room they shared, having at last got rid of Anne who had most importunately insisted upon hearing every detail of the adventure which the girls had been unable to recount before their aunt, neither was able to sleep.

'It was exceedingly unlucky that Lady Bourden and Amelia should have called here today,' Charlotte remarked.

'Yes. But it was very clever of you to tell about the smugglers without mentioning where we had been.'

'There is only one difficulty about that,' Charlotte remarked. 'If we do have to speak to the constable, he is sure to ask us what time we met the smugglers. Indeed, by tomorrow our aunt may have thought of it herself

— indeed, I am sure she will, and I am certain she is quite capable of keeping us locked up on bread and water for a week!'

'Oh, no!' Kitty assured her. 'Aunt Radley may sound very cross — but she has never done anything like that.'

'I hope you are right,' Charlotte returned doubtfully. 'But, oh, Kitty, was not it a splendid adventure!'

'I did not enjoy it at all!'

'Not while it was happening — but now that it is all over . . . '

'Do you find it so *very* dull here, Charlotte?'

'Oh, I love being with *you*, Kitty! But — you do not *do* very much here, do you?'

'There will be the ball at Pentallack next week.'

'Oh, and how I am looking forward to that, Kitty! It will be such fun to wear a ball gown again and to stand up with some delightful young men!' A sad thought suddenly struck Charlotte. 'I — I suppose you do *have* some delightful young men about here, Kitty?'

'Charlotte!' Kitty sounded scandalised.

'Well, it is young men who make for a lively ball, Kitty, mark my words. Oh, I suppose you will not mind who is there as long as you stand up with your cousin, Bob Pritchard, but — I must look out for myself.'

'Tom will present his friends to you, Charlotte.'

'That will be very agreeable,' Charlotte returned, having absolutely no faith in the elegance of her cousin Tom's acquaintances.

The two girls lay quietly for some moments, then Kitty said slowly, 'Charlotte, this evening — when the smugglers caught us ... do you remember that one of them had a — a very cultured voice?'

'Yes, I think so,' Charlotte answered after a moment's thought. 'He asked Tregarth what was the matter.'

'Yes, that's right. Well,' Kitty went on,

'I am not *quite* sure, Charlotte, but I am almost sure that I have heard that voice before!'

'Kitty! What do you mean? Who's voice was it?'

'I do not remember. I have been trying to think.'

'Oh, Kitty! You must remember! Could one of your friends possibly be a smuggler?'

'I — I do not think so . . . ' Kitty returned doubtfully.

'Kitty, you *must* remember! Oh, what a lark! And there was a French voice also! Do you remember, Kitty, after the voice had spoken to Tregarth, he spoke in French and was answered in French.'

'Oh, Charlotte! Do you think he could have been a — a spy?'

'Kitty! I did not think of it at the time, I was so frightened. But perhaps you are right. It is not far to Falmouth, is it, and the packet leaves from there for the West Indies — '

'I am not sure that one man would find out much there. But he might make his way to Plymouth where there are many of our Navy ships . . . '

The girls talked over this possibility for some minutes. It was not, after all, such a very far-fetched idea. England had been at war with the new French Republic for a little more than two years, and in any coastal area there were always many alarms of enemy descents upon the coast and of the infiltration of spies, all too likely on an isolated, wild coast such as there was about St. Bride's. It was not surprising that Kitty had been more aware of the possibility than Charlotte.

'But — would Englishmen, even smugglers — bring in a spy?' Charlotte queried.

'I am afraid that they would do anything for money!' Kitty returned.

'Oh, Kitty! You *must* remember to whom that voice belongs! Why — we may all be murdered in our beds . . . '

'I will try! I will try!'

A few moments later Charlotte got out of bed and went to the window to adjust the curtain which was allowing a brilliant beam of moonlight to fall across the bed. As she pulled the curtains together, Charlotte thought she noticed a movement in the vicarage garden and peeped out.

Her astonishment at what she saw was intense, and she almost yelped, 'Kitty, come here!'

'What is it?' Kitty scrambled out of bed and joined her cousin at the window. She saw nothing at all which should not have been there. 'I can not see anything!'

'Wait!' Charlotte hissed. 'In those bushes — on the right.'

'But — what is it?'

'Just watch.'

The girls waited in silence for some minutes, then Kitty said, 'I am going back to bed, Charlotte. I can not see what you mean.' And she turned away.

Charlotte grabbed her arm. 'Kitty! Look!' she whispered excitedly.

The other girl looked out of the

window again. Emerging from the bushes was a dark figure carrying a spade. Quite unconscious that he was being watched, the figure crossed the open grass and disappeared round the front of the house.

The two girls stared at each other, then slowly Charlotte put the curtain back in place.

'Oh, Charlotte!' Kitty breathed.

Her cousin gazed at her, for once totally lost for any words. Both girls had recognised the figure immediately. There could be no doubt that the slightly-stooped shoulders belonged to the vicar of St. Bride's himself.

★ ★ ★

In the morning, Tom Radley came in to breakfast, full of plans to call out the militia to find the smugglers' haul. 'I thought I'd ride over to see Captain Bidder,' he said. 'What do you think, sir?' he asked his father.

'I dare say the revenue men have it all

30

in hand,' the vicar answered absently.

'But if Tom can give information to catch the villains, it would be very desirable,' Miss Radley remarked.

'Perhaps you are right, my dear,' the vicar returned.

Charlotte and Kitty looked at each other silently.

'You had better ask the captain to return with you to question Catherine and Charlotte himself,' Miss Radley said, directing a sharp glance at the two girls.

'But we told everything last night, ma'am,' Charlotte said. 'Tom can tell this Captain Bidder. We can add nothing to what we have said already!'

'You need not fear, niece,' Miss Radley said blandly. '*I*, of course, will chaperone you.'

Charlotte looked down at her plate, wondering if the full extent of their escapade was now to be revealed to their aunt. Tom's next remark fell unpleasantly on her ears.

'By the way, Kitty,' he said, 'does this

belong to you? I found it in my pocket this morning. I can not think how it got there.' And he held up a lace-edged handkerchief.

'It — it is mine, Tom,' Charlotte said, decidedly discomfited.

'Yours, Charlotte! But how on earth — '

'I suppose you must have picked it up somewhere,' Charlotte returned nonchalantly, while silently blaming herself for her carelessness in not clearing the pockets of the coat she had borrowed.

Luckily, Miss Radley's attention had been occupied by the two younger boys at that moment, and she made no comment.

After breakfast the family dispersed, Anne and the younger boys going for lessons with their father, and Miss Radley about household affairs. Charlotte detained Kitty till the others were all gone; then she picked up the fire shovel and said firmly, 'Come on, Kitty!'

'Where? And why are you taking the shovel?'

'We are going to look in those bushes!'

'Oh, no, Charlotte!'

'Oh, yes! There's a mystery there, Kitty, and I mean to find it out!'

'I would rather not!'

'Then you need not come,' Charlotte returned determinedly, and made for the door.

Kitty followed unwillingly.

Concealing the shovel in the folds of her gown, Charlotte crossed the hall and was soon outside. Kitty caught up with her, and swiftly the two made for the clump of bushes from which they had seen the vicar emerge.

'Now we should be able to see where the earth has been disturbed,' Charlotte said quietly.

'How do we know it will have been disturbed?'

'My uncle was carrying a spade!'

The girls hunted about for a few minutes, Kitty very half-heartedly. But

Charlotte was not long in finding what she was looking for.

'This looks like the spot!' she said excitedly, and began to poke the earth with the fire shovel.

'Oh, Charlotte! I do wish you would not!'

'Well, we are hardly likely to find a body, are we?' Charlotte remarked reasonably.

After a very little digging, the girl unearthed a small wooden cask. She turned to look at her cousin with wide eyes, then knelt down upon the earth and sniffed.

'What is it?' Kitty whispered, almost in tears.

'It is as I thought!' Charlotte pronounced triumphantly. 'It is brandy!'

'You mean — ?' Kitty gasped, unable to continue.

'It must be so, Kitty. It seems that my uncle is in league with the smugglers!'

2

Captain Bidder duly appeared that morning to question the two girls about their encounter with the smugglers. Miss Radley sat there stiff-backed, once more suspicious, and looking keenly from one niece to the other as the captain's questions were answered.

It was Charlotte who did most of the talking, Kitty being quite unable to raise her voice above a whisper. Charlotte answered calmly, giving an estimate of the number of donkeys they had heard, the likely size of the smuggling party and other such matters.

But there really was little that could be told. By great good fortune, when the captain enquired as to times, Charlotte was vague, and when pressed, she was just about to confess that they had not met the smugglers till dusk had fallen, when Miss Radley was summoned to the kitchen to see a fallen blancmange or some such matter, and she was able to make her confession with only Tom to hear her.

'But, Charlotte, you said — !' he burst out.

Charlotte looked loftily at her cousin. 'We had no wish to worry our aunt,' she broke in. She turned back to the captain. 'There is one more thing, sir, that may be of interest. One of the smugglers had a very cultured voice, and my cousin believes that she has heard it before. This voice spoke in French, and was also answered in that language. We thought, of course, that it might be a spy.'

This piece of information was of far greater interest to Captain Bidder than the details of the smugglers that the girls had provided. Both Tom and the captain questioned them closely about the Frenchmen, but they could supply nothing more of interest. By the time Miss Radley returned, the smugglers had been well nigh forgotten, and when the captain departed, Tom went with him, and no whisper reached Miss Radley of their clandestine trip to Trevannock Fair.

Charlotte, unlike Kitty, was left in a whirl of excitement, and every time she left the vicarage, she kept a sharp lookout both for smugglers and French spies. She delighted to tell her aunt's callers of what had befallen Kitty and herself, and if the story was enhanced a little at each telling, it gave the hearers and herself greater pleasure. She accepted the condolences on the fright and discomfort she and Kitty had endured with aplomb, and felt almost insulted if other subjects were introduced during the calls.

She had hoped, of course, for further adventures at once, and was consequently the more disappointed when the days went by, and absolutely nothing of interest happened to break the renewed monotony. Life was excessively tame, she sighed; it was not at all what she had hoped for when she came into Cornwall, and there was nothing but the Pentallack ball to depend upon now.

★ ★ ★

The party of five from the St. Bride's vicarage arrived at Pentallack without mishap. Charlotte was looking her best, as she always did when any pleasure was in the offing: her eyes shining, and a becoming pink tinting her cheeks. Kitty looked very pretty also, but in a more demure way, though she was no less excited than her cousin because she knew she would have at least one dance with her cousin on her mother's side, Bob Pritchard.

When the party arrived, they were greeted by Lord and Lady Pentallack, then made their way to the circle round the fire where Miss Radley greeted her cronies, presented Charlotte to those who did not know her already, and settled herself comfortably next to Lady

Bourden, and prepared for a good cose. Amelia Bourden was standing beside her mother; the three girls at once fell into conversation, looking about the room for future agreeable partners. Mr. Radley made his way at once to the card-room, and Tom abandoned his womenfolk to join his friends, walking up and down the room, and quizzing the female beauties paraded for their benefit that evening, as young men in their early twenties think their right.

When the dancing started, all three young ladies were led out without delay, and for the next hour, therefore, being in different sets, Charlotte and Kitty had no opportunity to speak together. Then they met briefly beside Miss Radley's chair when the first dances were over, and Kitty had just time to whisper, 'Charlotte, I must speak with you!' when Bob Pritchard appeared, and Kitty had no eyes for anyone else.

Charlotte sighed and curbed her curiosity as best she could, but her own attention was shortly absorbed when her cousin Tom very unexpectedly appeared before her, begging leave to present a tall, dark and exceedingly handsome young man who had apparently requested the introduction.

'Charlotte, this is the Marquis de MontSauvage,' Tom said. 'He has recently escaped from those murdering Frenchies and has sought refuge with us. He knows no-one here, and as you do not know people either, I thought you might stand up together.'

Charlotte was by no means averse to this, and smiled graciously, and most willingly walked beside the young Frenchman to take their places in the set that was then forming, her mind full of the words of the gypsy at Trevannock fair. She had certainly not expected such a partner from her cousin Tom.

'You have come but recently to England, sir, I think my cousin said?' she asked, anxious to know more of this very interesting young man.

'That is correct, Mademoiselle,' he

returned in a voice made even more delightful by its intriguing foreign accent. He smiled down charmingly, and Charlotte felt her heart flutter quite distinctly in her breast.

'How did you manage to escape, sir? Were you in very great danger?'

'Oh, yes! They were very anxious to deprive me of my head!' the marquis replied with a wry smile.

'I am very glad indeed that they did not, sir!'

M. MontSauvage bowed. 'And I, Mademoiselle!'

'How did you manage to escape, sir?' Charlotte pursued.

'My home is in Brittany, Mademoiselle. I was able to escape by sea,' the Frenchman smiled. 'Luckily, my servants were still faithful, and I was given warning in advance of my arrest, and I was able to escape at once. It is very difficult to be a nobleman in France now.'

'So we have heard, sir,' Charlotte returned, exquisitely sorry for this handsome young man, so nearly deprived of life. 'After your King, and then your Queen were guillotined, it seemed that nothing could be more terrible. But now, we hear, blood flows daily in the streets, and hundreds are put to the blade. I am exceedingly thankful that we have our Channel to protect us.'

'And now I too am thankful for *La Manche*, Mademoiselle.'

'*La Manche*? Oh, yes; of course; that is your name for the English Channel.'

M. MontSauvage smiled again, but then the music began and Charlotte had no opportunity for further questions. She was acutely conscious that she was dancing with one of the most attractive men in the room. When they reached the bottom of the set, however, Charlotte was able to pursue the conversation.

'And your family, sir? Are they all safe?'

The marquis's face clouded at once, but he said briefly, 'My sister — she is still in Brittany, Mademoiselle.' But he said it in such a way that it was clear that he did not wish to speak of the matter. Tactfully Charlotte went on to speak of other things, determined to make the best impression on the elegant Frenchman.

At the end of these two dances, Charlotte and Kitty met again.

'You wanted to speak with me, Kitty?' Charlotte demanded, putting a hand on her cousin's arm, dragging her thoughts away from the marquis with some difficulty.

'Oh! Yes! Oh, Charlotte!' Kitty's face which had been smiling and dimpled with pleasure after her dances with her cousin Bob, now grew earnest. 'Charlotte, something has happened!' Kitty's voice grew excited. 'Oh, you will never guess!'

'Then tell me quickly!'

Kitty looked about her quickly, then taking her cousin's arm, she said, 'Let us go to one of the withdrawing rooms.'

The two girls linked arms and made

43

their way across the room together. They made a delightful pair: Charlotte taller than her cousin, with abundant chestnut hair and deep blue eyes, and vivacious manner; and Kitty, quieter, all pink and white, and blonde curls, and a very sweet expression when she was not worried about anything. There were a good many pairs of young male eyes which watched them with more than common interest.

When they were upstairs, Kitty led the way to one of the rooms which had been set aside for the use of the ladies, made sure that there was no-one within, then drew her cousin inside and closed the door.

'Now, Kitty, what is it?' Charlotte demanded, filled with curiosity.

'You remember that voice we heard when the smugglers caught us? The cultured one, I mean?' Kitty demanded with shining eyes.

'Yes!'

'Well, I am sure I have heard it again this evening!'

'Kitty! Whose is it?'

'Lord Pentallack's son; Richard Tregelles.'

'Kitty! It — it can not be! You must be mistaken!'

Kitty shook her head. 'I am sure I am not. I stood next to him in the first set. He spoke to me. I am quite certain that I am not mistaken!'

Charlotte thought this over for several moments. 'But — what on earth would Lord Pentallack's son be doing with the smugglers?' she objected.

'My father had a keg of brandy from them,' Kitty returned unhappily.

'Yes. But I understand that a great many perfectly respectable people in this part of the country do have dealings with the smugglers. I did not realise it before, and it certainly would not do in Shropshire, but I heard Aunt Radley say the other day that old Miss Tregear had had her lace brought in by smugglers, and she looks a law-abiding body enough!' Charlotte spoke hurriedly, hoping not to upset her cousin.

'I mean, I could understand it if Richard Tregelles had received some wine or brandy from the smugglers, but — I can not think — I mean, surely he would not actually *go* with them!'

'I am certain that I am not mistaken,' Kitty repeated with gentle obstinacy. 'You have not met Mr. Tregelles, have you? Well, I will present him, then you may hear for yourself.'

'I do not know that I would recognise the voice again,' Charlotte said doubtfully.

'Well, at least you may meet Mr. Tregelles.'

The girls made their way down to the ballroom again. As luck would have it, Tom Radley was in conversation with their host's son, and Kitty made her way to her brother immediately, Charlotte for once following.

'Tom, Charlotte has not yet made the acquaintance of Mr. Tregelles.'

Tom, not best pleased at having his conversation interrupted by the women of his family, performed the necessary introduction.

'Miss Radley, I regret that we have not met before,' Mr. Tregelles said smiling. 'I must have been settling my old aunt when you arrived.' He turned to Kitty. 'I must thank you, Miss Kitty, for repairing such an omission.' Then Mr. Tregelles turned back to Charlotte. That his eyes were admiring, for once Charlotte missed. She was far too busy wondering if she had heard his voice before. She was conscious of Kitty watching her with suppressed excitement. 'And how are you liking Cornwall, ma'am?' she heard Mr. Tregelles say now.

'Very well, I thank you, sir.'

'Oh, Charlotte!' Tom said with a laugh. 'What my cousin really means, Dick, is that she has found Cornwall excessively dull so far. From what we hear, it seems that Shropshire must be the liveliest county in the kingdom!'

'I am indeed sorry, Miss Radley, that you have found it so,' Mr. Tregelles said with concern. 'But, am not I correct, ma'am, in thinking that you and Miss Kitty have had an exceedingly unpleasant encounter with smugglers?'

'We did indeed, sir!' Charlotte returned, looking somewhat suspiciously at Mr. Tregelles. His face was perfectly grave, but the fact that he had mentioned the girls' meeting with the smugglers only seemed to confirm Kitty's words. 'But my cousin exaggerates,' she went on smiling. 'However, I must tell you that we do have an exceedingly lively neighbourhood at home.'

'Then we must try to change your opinion of Cornwall, Miss Charlotte. Now that the spring is come, we must arrange some excursions for you. There are so many beautiful places to see. And our French guest must be shown the country also. Perhaps we could make up a party together, Tom?'

'Your *French* guest, sir?' In something of a daze, Charlotte recalled the French voice she had heard that night at Melyn Cove, then her thoughts flew to the elegant foreigner with whom she had so recently been dancing.

'Yes, Charlotte!' Tom said a trifle impatiently. 'You remember, I presented you. You stood up with him!'

'Oh, yes, of course! Monsieur Mont-Sauvage,' Charlotte gasped, glancing quickly at Kitty. All was plain to her in a trice. Mr. Tregelles had gone out with the smugglers to rescue his friend, the marquis, from the French guillotine! How foolish of them not to think of it before! 'I — I collect that M. MontSauvage has but recently come to England, sir?' she said hastily.

'Yes; he has been here but a bare se'ennight.'

Charlotte and Kitty exchanged glances at that.

'He — mentioned that he had escaped by sea, sir,' Charlotte pursued.

'Yes,' Mr. Tregelles answered easily. 'I tell him that he was exceedingly lucky that the spring gales are past early this year. I am afraid my friend is no sailor, and our coast is very treacherous in all but the best weather.'

'W — where did he land, sir?' Charlotte made herself ask. She felt Kitty's eyes were large and round as they gazed at her now. Her own she kept firmly on Mr. Tregelles' face.

'At the very spot, ma'am, where you had your encounter with the smugglers: at Melyn Cove.'

'Oh!' Charlotte gasped faintly.

'Our families are old friends, and the marquis knew that he could find a home with us.'

Tom burst out, laughing as at a good joke. 'It is lucky, then, that he did not meet your smugglers as he came in, is it not, Charlotte? I do not suppose the smugglers would have been as gentle with a man as they were with two females!'

'Very likely you are right!' Charlotte got out.

Kitty was quite beyond speech now.

Charlotte saw that Mr. Tregelles was regarding her with an air of puzzled amusement. He might not have yet realised that the two young men the smugglers had taken were indeed herself and Kitty, but, surely it could not be long before he had thought out the truth. The true enormity of their escapade was no longer safe.

Hurriedly she turned to Mr. Tregelles, and asked, though at the moment she could not have been less interested, 'Pray tell me, sir, where are the best beauty spots about here? I should dearly like to go upon some excursions to see the countryside.'

As she spoke, she was wondering how on earth she could beg Mr. Tregelles to keep their secret still.

'We must certainly arrange some picnics to our best areas, Miss Charlotte,' Mr. Tregelles was saying. 'But, if you would do me the honour of standing up with me for the next pair of dances, I would hope to persuade you further of the delights of my county.'

Still in something of a daze, Charlotte allowed herself to be led out by

Mr. Tregelles. They took their places some way down the set, and conversation was therefore incumbent upon them. Never had Charlotte wanted to speak so urgently, and never had words come so laggardly to her lips. She thought that she must make one more attempt to discover if Mr. Tregelles did indeed suspect the truth.

'Did — did M. MontSauvage — come to England alone?' she enquired as innocently as she was able.

Immediately she thought that Mr. Tregelles was smiling at her in a most odious manner.

But the answer came calmly, 'Mademoiselle MontSauvage, the marquis's sister, is yet in France.'

'Indeed?'

'I am afraid so.'

'But why did not she — ?'

'Escape with M. MontSauvage? I am afraid I do not know, ma'am. And now, of course, MontSauvage is constantly worried for her safety.'

'But — perhaps she may yet escape

— by the same means!'

It seemed to Charlotte that Mr. Tregelles gave a swift, shrewd glance at her before replying with a smile, 'It is to be hoped so, ma'am!'

'It is very strange, is it not,' Charlotte dared, almost holding her breath, 'that my cousin and I should have been at the very spot — on the very day — when M. MontSauvage arrived here?'

'When you were taken by the smugglers, you mean? It is indeed, ma'am!'

Charlotte had the uncomfortable feeling that Mr. Tregelles was laughing at her, and she felt exceedingly annoyed with the young man. 'Did *you* help M. MontSauvage to escape?' she demanded bluntly.

'*I*, ma'am?'

'Yes, you, sir!'

'I — have no means of getting into France, ma'am. And I should have no liking to being taken as a spy!'

Charlotte stared at the young man

53

with smouldering eyes. Mr. Tregelles and the marquis, she judged, were about the same age, in their late twenties, she thought; both were tall and dark, and she supposed that some would consider Mr. Tregelles also handsome. There could be no doubt that the marquis was. But whereas the foreigner was all charm and chivalry, Mr. Tregelles was odiously superior, and Charlotte was convinced that he was laughing at her. Oh, it was too bad! But — if Mr. Tregelles knew her secret, Charlotte was sure that she had found out his own, which was some small satisfaction.

'No. I suppose a spy would be shown no mercy,' Charlotte returned shortly. 'Nor would smugglers, I should imagine!'

'I am sure you are right, Miss Charlotte!'

It was their turn to dance up the set, then, and the conversation was left in this unsatisfactory manner, and when it was resumed after their turn, Mr.

Tregelles started determinedly speaking of the places Charlotte should see during her holiday in Cornwall, and she had no opportunity to resume their former subject.

Later in the evening she was delighted to stand up again with M. MontSauvage, but she had no more success in getting him to admit that he had been brought from France by smugglers. In any case, Charlotte did not press the matter too far, as she had no wish for the Frenchman to learn that she had been so immodest as to appear in public, disguised in male attire. At the time, it had seemed a good joke; now, she would have given a good deal to have the escapade undone.

When she and Kitty were alone in their room that night, they talked round every aspect of the topic of the smugglers and the marquis and Mr. Tregelles. Both girls were convinced that it was Mr. Tregelles and the marquis they had heard that night at Melyn Cove.

'I do not understand why Mr. Tregelles would not admit it?' Charlotte said, puzzled.

'I expect the smugglers swore them to secrecy. And — if they hope to rescue Mademoiselle MontSauvage by the same means, then they must certainly do as the smugglers tell them,' Kitty returned.

'I daresay you are right, my love.'

'And at least Mr. Tregelles, even if he guesses that we were the young men, will not be able to say anything about it.'

'Not to Aunt Radley, perhaps,' was Charlotte's rueful reply, which she did not elaborate to her cousin.

* * *

Mr. Tregelles was as good as his word. In the next few days invitations came to the St. Bride's vicarage for excursions and musical evenings, dinners and card suppers, and there were even one or two impromptu dances. Charlotte was not only gratified, but very delighted that M. MontSauvage paid her a good deal of attention, and always asked her to stand up with him for the first dance.

His attentions were such that after only a few days, Kitty asked her cousin if she had a *tendre* for the Frenchman.

'Oh, Kitty! I — I *do* like him exceedingly,' Charlotte exclaimed, never having felt in the least like this before. 'I must confess that I do not know any young man whom I have liked more . . . ' She paused and blushed. 'Perhaps . . . perhaps I am — a little in love with him!' And she laughed uncertainly.

'Oh, Charlotte! I am so happy for you!' Being in love herself, Kitty wished all around her to be in the same happy state, and was delighted that her cousin seemed in a fair way to following in her own footsteps. 'You do not find Cornwall so *very* dull, now!'

'No, indeed! I do not find it dull at all!' Charlotte declared frankly. 'But — I have not the least idea how M. MontSauvage may feel!'

'Surely you can not doubt that he likes you very well, Charlotte! Why, I have never seen anyone more attentive!'

Charlotte smiled, well content.

There had been nothing in Mr. Tregelles' conduct to make her change her mind about him. Though he was always perfectly polite, and certainly she was grateful to him for the efforts he had put into planning schemes for her amusement, yet she was always conscious that he held her — and Kitty's — secret, and always she suspected that he was laughing at her clandestinely. She supposed it would seem a good joke to think that two well-brought-up young ladies had dared to appear in breeches, and her only hope was that he had not told anyone of his suspicions, in order to guard his own secret of his dependence on the smugglers for M. MontSauvage's safety. But, as she regretfully thought, there could be no dependence that he had not told M. MontSauvage himself.

However, it seemed that Mr. Tregelles must have said nothing so far, for the marquis was never anything but absolutely agreeable and attentive. Indeed, that very evening, Charlotte was most happy to bask in the company of the delightful young Frenchman, acutely aware of every flattering phrase, every melting look, that he directed at her.

'Your dress, Mademoiselle, it is *ravissante*. It has quite the French line. I did not expect to find such fashion in England.'

'You are very kind, sir,' Charlotte dimpled.

'I speak only the truth, Mademoiselle. But then, since the moment I first saw you, I saw at once that you had the style of a French woman. And a beauty that is English,' he added, and directed at Charlotte a very speaking look.

Charlotte's heart fluttered delightfully. 'Oh, indeed, sir, you flatter me!'

'Not at all, Mademoiselle! I have admired you from the very first time we met — and how could I not! I saw you across the room, and demanded that your cousin Tom present me. Ah, Mademoiselle! Such style! Such grace! Such — modesty!'

Charlotte looked down, much pleased, but slightly doubtful of the last compliment. After all, she could not remember ever suffering from shyness; how very unfortunate if the marquis was attracted to retiring females . . .

But the marquis was continuing warmly. 'In exile as I am, Mademoiselle, torn from my home, my family, my friends — all that I have hitherto held dear, it is *you*, Mademoiselle, who have made all supportable for me! You have been my first friend here, Mademoiselle, and without you, my life would be barren indeed . . .'

Charlotte smiled her pleasure, and M. MontSauvage took her hand and held it for a moment, pressing it tenderly, and looking at her most speakingly.

Certainly I *must* be growing into love

with him, Charlotte thought to herself. All this must be something more than mere flirtation.

Mr. Tregelles came up to them then, and the delightful tête-à-tête was ended. Mr. Tregelles, Charlotte thought somewhat heatedly, never paid her any compliments at all. His politeness and liveliness never varied, but — there were no speaking looks, no flirtatious compliments. Sometimes, Charlotte thought, he almost treated her in the same teasing way as did her cousin Tom. Still, she was grateful to him for arranging the excursions and other schemes which had suddenly made her stay in Cornwall so much more agreeable.

One day a party was made up to visit some aged, mysterious stones on the other side of the county. There were three great, upright stones supporting an even more gigantic one, like a tabletop.

'Can not you imagine, Miss Charlotte, the white-robed Druids cutting up their human sacrifices on that great top stone?' Mr. Tregelles had demanded with a laugh.

Charlotte grimaced, while Kitty and Amelia Bourden squealed.

'Oh, do not think my cousin Charlotte so easily affrighted, Dick!' Tom returned. 'Why, I quite believe that she would be able to outface any Druid that she might encounter!'

And Richard Tregelles had looked down at her with laughing grey eyes. 'You know that this is a wishing stone, Miss Charlotte?' he had added. 'Come, why do you not take advantage of the opportunity? You must walk under the stone three times, and then make your wish. It is of sovereign worth.'

Charlotte had looked somewhat doubtfully at the huge cross-stone.

'You need not worry that it will fall, ma'am,' Mr. Tregelles said quickly. 'Come, Tom, do you show your cousin . . . '

'No, no, I will go,' Charlotte said quickly. 'I am not afraid. I was just wondering what should be my wish.'

'Why do you not wish for more excitement while you are with us, Charlotte?' Tom laughed. 'After all, it is at least three weeks since your adventure with the smugglers!'

'Ah, yes, the smugglers!' Mr. Tregelles murmured with a smile.

Yet again Charlotte had the suspicion that he was laughing at her, and to hide her vexation, she began to walk under the stone quickly. When she had finished the ritual, she was glad to walk away with M. MontSauvage. His flattery was very soothing, and she liked it a good deal better than the teasing.

A day or so after this, Charlotte had the misfortune to twist her ankle quite severely, and she was forced to rest it upon a sofa. On the second evening after the accident, there was a small card-party at the vicarage, and while the others played, Charlotte rested her foot, and was reading when the marquis was announced.

Cards were interrupted while he greeted everyone, but were soon resumed, when M. MontSauvage came to sit near Charlotte.

'Tregelles asked me to give his apologies. He was not able to come tonight, but he was anxious to know how you are.'

'Please thank him, and say that I am very well. I hope to be walking as usual tomorrow — or certainly the next day.'

'Tregelles could not come — because he has business in hand!'

Charlotte thought the marquis looked quite excited. 'Oh?' she prompted.

'And such business, Mademoiselle!'

'I see that it pleases you also, sir!'

'Oh, it does, Mademoiselle! It does!' And the marquis regarded her with very speaking eyes. He resumed in a low voice, 'I am not supposed to say anything to anybody, but — I would like *you* to know, Mademoiselle.' And the marquis's eyes looked more melt-ingly than ever.

'Yes, sir?' Charlotte murmured, very curious.

'You, who have always been my friend — for whom I — ' The marquis stopped suddenly, tightening his lips, then continued after a moment, 'But no! I will say nothing till — till after what is to happen — has happened!' Then his voice dropped. 'You will promise to say nothing — not to nobody, Mademoiselle?' The marquis was urgent.

'Of course, sir!' Charlotte was curious in the extreme, and immensely flattered that the marquis should take her into his confidence.

'It is my sister, Mademoiselle!' the marquis whispered after a moment. 'Tregelles is gone to — to make arrangements for her to come to England. It is a great relief, Mademoiselle! You know how worried I have been for her . . . '

'I did not understand why your sister did not leave with you, sir.'

The marquis's face clouded. 'She

65

refused to come. My sister would not leave France!'

'Would not come! But — I do not understand — !'

The Frenchman was silent for some moments. Then he said slowly, 'It is very painful to me to speak of it, Mademoiselle. My sister is very young — barely sixteen, but — because our parents died when she was very young, she has not been controlled as she should have been. And so it happened that — the foolish girl thought she was in love with one of these — these regicides!'

'In love!' Charlotte gasped, looking appalled. 'Your sister was in love with one of those who sought your life?'

The marquis nodded sadly. 'She would not leave because of him, Mademoiselle. He is a worthless rogue! I have known him all my life! We were boys together. And he thinks now to abase my family by allying himself with my sister. And she, foolish creature . . . But now, I have had news that all is not well. This Marton is tired of her, and is paying attentions to someone else, and I have had word that Marie-Claire has been denounced. My friend, the Comte de Vauclou, has just escaped to England, and he has told me that my sister is in danger of the guillotine. So she must be brought out of France at once. Indeed, we may be too late already!'

'Oh, I do hope not, sir!'

M. MontSauvage nodded gloomily. 'Tregelles is gone — to the friends who brought me from France — '

'The smugglers, you mean, sir?' Charlotte said softly.

The marquis looked at her in surprise, then nodded. 'Yes, Mademoiselle. And it is only when Marie-Claire is safe, Miss Charlotte . . . ' And the Frenchman gave Charlotte another speaking look.

'And who is now caring for your sister, sir?'

'If she is still at home, there is our old nurse — and the servants. But I pray every day that we will not be too late. My sister is of a courage formidable, but — she is so young. My poor mother could not have supported these troubles for one moment. But then — she was an angel. A perfect woman. She moved only in the shadow of my father. But — perhaps luckily — my sister is not like that. But — she is not a woman I would wish to have for a wife!'

'No, sir?'

'*Mais non!* I must have — someone — like my mother.'

'Indeed, sir,' Charlotte murmured, her heart sinking into her slippers at the thought that she herself, she was certain, did not in the least resemble the late Marquise de MontSauvage.

But then the marquis gave her another very speaking look, and smiled so very delightfully, that Charlotte allowed her heart to rise again. And she wondered very often what it could possibly be that the marquis intended to do after his sister was safe. That he meant to do something, Charlotte was sure, for he had dropped so many hints; and that it concerned herself, she permitted herself to be almost equally certain.

She should, she thought some time later, feel some gratitude that Mr. Tregelles had clearly not mentioned to the marquis anything of his suspicions that Charlotte and Kitty had been the young men taken by the smugglers the night M. MontSauvage had come to England. But then, she thought defiantly, to do so would hardly have been the action of a gentleman . . .

3

Charlotte's ankle was perfectly recovered the next day, but any thought of going on any excursion was quite out of the question for the heavens had opened, and rain fell incessantly in thick, sheeting gusts. Whereas before the spring had been warm and agreeable, now the air was bleak and near freezing, and the daffodils and primroses were dashed to the earth by the furious weather.

There was nothing at all for Charlotte and Kitty to do but talk and read and sew, and at the end of the long day of ceaseless downpour, Charlotte quite envied her cousin Tom, who insisted that he had to go out despite the inclement times. Miss Radley sniffed, and looked disapproving, but it had been several years since she had had any control over Tom, and out he rode, despite her objections.

It was very late when he returned. The rain had ceased, but the wind howled louder than ever when he stumbled into the vicarage, coughing and limping sadly.

'I told you it was foolish to think of venturing forth!' Miss Radley said quite crossly, when Tom appeared. But at a second glance she rose, and went to her nephew swiftly and helped him to a chair. His clothes were very muddy, and his face was oddly white. 'What has happened?' Miss Radley demanded.

'My horse slipped and fell,' Tom gasped.

'You have injured yourself?'

'My leg,' Tom replied, wincing with pain.

The others had all gathered round, their faces grave with concern. It took but a few moments for Miss Radley to have her nephew carried to his room, undressed and put to bed. She then went to inspect the damage for herself.

When she came downstairs again, her

face looked grim. 'I fear his leg may be broken. We must summon the surgeon urgently in the morning, Mr. Radley.'

'Oh, poor Tom!' Kitty cried.

'He has no-one but himself to blame!' Miss Radley said tartly.

But it was Miss Radley who thought up delicate dishes to tempt the invalid's appetite, and who remained with him through the night to be on hand in case he should need anything.

Tom's leg was indeed broken, and Mr. Maker, the surgeon, came on the following day and set it. Fortunately, the break was a simple one, and the family were assured that as long as Tom was kept quiet, all might proceed very well. 'Certainly, his cough is a complication, but if fever can be kept away, I see no reason why young Mr. Radley should not mend in time.'

Tom himself slept most of the morning, and Miss Radley remained with him still. The household was unnaturally quiet, and Kitty wept a good deal, out of worry for her brother.

Charlotte, who had never particularly cared for Tom and his teasing, would now have given a good deal to have him laughing at her as he did so often.

Later in the day, however, Tom was awake and seemingly cheerful, and so much was he his usual self, that he prevailed upon Miss Radley to take a rest, and send the girls to him in her place.

'But you are not to excite him, mind!' their aunt told Charlotte and Kitty sternly. 'You are only to talk a little, and do not on any account excite him. You heard what Mr. Maker said: any excitement would be very bad for him.'

The girls promised obedience, and tiptoed into the room. Kitty was sadly frightened when she saw her brother's flushed face, but was somewhat reassured when he spoke with a sufficient measure of his old ebullience.

After Tom had assured both girls that he did well enough, he asked Kitty if she would go to look for a particular book in the library and bring it to him.

'You want to read, brother!'

'I must do something, Kitty! And a book on the Godolphin Arabian will do as well as any.'

As Kitty walked to the door, Tom winked at Charlotte, and as his sister closed the door behind her, he grinned, and said in a satisfied voice, 'That should take her sufficient time!'

'Tom! What are you about?' Charlotte demanded in a whisper.

'I must speak to you, cousin,' he returned in an urgent whisper.

'What is it?'

'Charlotte, you must help me!'

'Of course I will! What is it? What can I get you?'

'I want you to do something for me, Charlotte! There is no-one else I can ask!' And now Tom leaned up on one elbow, and grasped Charlotte's arm, with a look of urgent appeal in his eyes.

'Of course I will, Tom. But — '

'Oh, Charlotte! Do listen! I may have only a few moments — '

Charlotte was about to speak, but

Tom silenced her with an exasperated look.

'Listen, Charlotte! Tonight — but first, you must promise absolute secrecy.'

'Oh, very well! What is it?'

'You promise?'

'I have said so!'

'Well, tonight; they are to go to France to attempt to bring out MontSauvage's sister.'

'It is tonight!' Charlotte exclaimed.

Tom looked astonished. 'You knew of it?'

'M. MontSauvage mentioned that they were to try soon.'

'I see; well — I am supposed to go with them, Charlotte, but of course that is impossible now. Will you take a message to Tregelles, Charlotte, saying that I can not join them? I am indeed sorry to put this upon you, Charlotte, but you will see that there is no-one else whom I may ask. It must be done in the greatest secrecy. If wind of the voyage should get out, then they may

75

refuse to go — '

'The smugglers you mean, Tom?' Charlotte whispered.

Tom gave her an odd look, but nodded. 'They are to leave upon the tide — at a little after seven.'

'But I could never get to Pentallack in the time, Tom! It is near five now!'

Tom's face fell, and he looked distressed. 'How long have I been asleep, then?'

'All the morning, Tom. We finished dinner before Kitty and I came to you!'

Tom let fall a forceful expletive, then apologised to his cousin. 'I am sorry, but — I can not think now what should be done. Tregelles must know that I am prevented from coming. I could not bear that he should think that I had let him down!'

Charlotte thought frantically. She could quite see Tom's point, and the plans to rescue Mademoiselle Mont-Sauvage might have to be altered if he were not part of the expedition.

'Perhaps,' she began doubtfully, ' — perhaps — if I took a message directly to the boat, I would at least reach them before they sailed,' she whispered. 'I know it would not be possible then for the plans to be rearranged, but at least they would know, Tom — '

Tom was seized then with a fit of coughing, and it was a few minutes before he could speak.

'Do you think you could do it, Charlotte?' he asked doubtfully at last.

'Have you any other idea?'

Tom thought for a moment. 'Are you sure you would not mind?'

'I suppose I may depend upon Mr. Tregelles to save me from the smugglers?'

Tom grinned.

'Tell me where I should go, then!'

'They are to sail from Melyn Cove.'

'Well, that is not too far! And at least I may walk there in the light.'

'It will be dusk when they sail, and you must return alone!'

'Now, do not worry about me, Tom! I shall be very well!' Charlotte said firmly, deciding that she would take a cudgel with her at the very least.

'You are a real go-er, cousin Charlotte!' Tom said admiringly. 'Still, you have always said that you like adventures . . .'

Charlotte grinned a little uncertainly, but agreed that she was getting her wish at last.

'Not a word to anyone, mind!' Tom urged. 'Not even to Kitty!'

'Very well.'

Charlotte was now considerably exercised in her mind as to how she could slip unseen from the house. It would take her a little less than half an hour to walk to Melyn Cove, but she decided she must give herself longer in case of mishap. That left her barely half an hour before she must set out. The rain of the previous day had stopped, but a sea-fret was blowing inland and the dark would descend early.

She had left Kitty with Tom, saying

78

that she had the headache and was going to lie down. Kitty had been all concern, but Charlotte had assured her that a little rest was all she needed. She longed to take Kitty into her confidence, but she had promised Tom that she would not, and so she had to make all plans alone. She had no liking for her mission, but she had promised Tom; and besides, she was glad to do even so small a thing to help the marquis. Still, at least she did not have to go to Pentallack and ask for Mr. Tregelles. There was no way in which she could have done that without its appearing exceedingly — odd.

It did not take her long to decide that she must perform her errand once more clad in male garments. She was somewhat exercised as to how she could get hold of Tom's clothes without being found out, but then she remembered that the muddy clothes Tom had worn the previous day had been brushed and cleaned and were now awaiting minor repairs in the sewing room.

Peeping out into the passage, Charlotte scampered along till she reached the little room, seized hold of shirt and jacket and breeches, looked for hose that might suit her, and luckily found Tom's riding boots also there. Hurrying back to her room, Charlotte locked the door, and changed hastily. Then she scribbled a note to Kitty, saying merely that she had had go out, but that she should be returned by half-past seven of the clock, and that she was not to worry; then she swung herself out of the window again, and sought for footholds as she made her way carefully down the ivy.

The mist was swirling round the vicarage, and was damp on Charlotte's face. Because of it, the light was already much lessened, and she had little fear of being seen as she reached the ground, and ran across the lawn to the wall, and out of the side gate.

In the lane the girl stopped and

strained her ears for sounds of movement. But in the mist all was quiet. It seemed as if the chickens and the animals had already gone to rest. Slowly Charlotte made her way into the lane and walked in the direction of the sea and Melyn Cove. At first she walked on tiptoe, fearful of breaking the silence; then she moved onto the grass at the side of the track, and struck out more boldly, gaining in confidence with every step she took away from the vicarage. She could easily get to Melyn Cove, give Mr. Tregelles the message, and be returned to St. Bride's by half-past seven.

Only then did it strike her that Mr. Tregelles would have to see her, dressed as she was; but there was no help for it, and Charlotte shrugged her shoulders bravely, and thought that she did not care one jot what Mr. Tregelles thought of her.

She encountered one or two labourers at the edge of the village, returning home for the night. Charlotte bade them goodnight as she passed them, and went on her way, thinking that she was making good progress, and that Tom would be pleased with her.

The shapes of gorse bushes and stunted trees loomed up out of the mist, and sometimes they made Charlotte jump. Once or twice a wandering cow, curious to discover what was going on, walked beside her for some steps, before turning off into the field again to look for new and greener grass. And sometimes a small group of goonhillies, the little local ponies, would move away as she approached.

The smell of the sea grew stronger as Charlotte neared her destination, and she struck out cheerfully. There was still enough light for her to avoid bumping into things, and she was certain that she had not much farther to go.

It was then that she heard the sound of raucous singing. A man's voice was raised in strident song, bidding farewell to Spanish ladies. Charlotte stopped in her tracks, trying to decide from exactly where the sound came. The voice died away, then began afresh, sounding nearer.

Charlotte peered about, rather alarmed. She had no wish to encounter a drunken stranger so near to her goal, and hoped that she might make her way round him, without being seen.

The singing died away once more, and Charlotte looked hard into the mist, straining her ears to catch the sound of footsteps. But all was still. Abruptly Charlotte felt frightened, and wished that she had remembered to bring a stout stick with her as she had planned.

Suddenly she felt a heavy hand on her shoulder, and a drunken voice roared close to her ear, 'Lost too, are ye, boy? In this God-forsaken hole?'

'Er — no — I live near here,' Charlotte managed to utter, feeling very much frightened.

'You sure?' the man demanded, squinting into her face. 'Didn' think anyone lived hereabouts.' Bloodshot eyes regarded her blearily, and Charlotte drew back at the smell of brandy which hit her like a wave.

'There's the village a little farther on,' Charlotte got out, gesturing behind her. 'I dare say you could get a bed for the night there.'

She tried to free herself from the hand on her shoulder, but the man clung to her.

'You come wi' me, boy,' he said. 'I don' like being by myself.'

'I — I am afraid that I am upon an errand, sir,' Charlotte said politely, anxious not to antagonise the man.

'I'll come wi' you, then. Where are ye goin'?'

'I'm taking a message to — to my uncle who farms this way.'

The man stood swaying, holding onto Charlotte's shoulder. 'Is it far?' he demanded after a moment.

'A few miles,' Charlotte got out.

'Don' like bein' alone,' the man whimpered, and began to cry, hanging onto both Charlotte's shoulders now.

'You're my frien'. Don' leave me!'

'I really am very sorry, sir, but — I must deliver my message,' Charlotte said, more firmly now, believing the man to be harmless.

'Don' leave me alone! Don' leave me alone!' the man begged.

'Look.' Charlotte felt in the pockets of Tom's coat, and then in the breeches' pocket. By great good luck she found a coin inside. She pulled it out. 'Look. You take this, sir. The village is only a very short distance away. There is a good inn there — where you may get some of the very best brandy you'll find in these parts.' And she held the coin out to the drunken man, but at some distance from him.

He put out his hand to take it, could not quite reach it, then took a step away from Charlotte to grasp it, letting go the girl's shoulder as he did so.

Charlotte sprang away at once, and ran in the direction of the cliff as fast as she could. Behind her she heard the man crying 'Don' leave me! Don' leave me! Don' like bein' alone!'

She feared that the man might come after her, but he did not, and in a few moments more, she heard his voice again raised in song, gradually growing fainter.

In another moment or two, Charlotte made out the edge of the cliff. She peered over carefully, but she could see nothing for the mist; but she heard the sound of the water rattling the stones on the shore.

★ ★ ★

Having followed the path from the village to Melyn Cove, she knew that the narrow track down to the beach must be somewhere to her left. Carefully she groped her way forward, frightened of pitching over the edge of the cliff onto the rocks below, and concerned now that she had little time left. But at last she recognised the huge rock, in the shade of which she and Kitty had hidden when they had come upon the smugglers, and knew that the path down to the cove must be very near at hand.

A moment later she heard quiet, quick footsteps behind her, and startled, she crouched near a gorse bush, hoping that she had not been seen.

'Who's there?' a rough voice demanded quietly.

Charlotte remained silent, holding her breath.

The man stopped for some moments, obviously listening, and then, to Charlotte's relief, she heard him move forward to the cliff edge, then disappear down the path to the cove.

Waiting till the man must have been near the bottom, Charlotte followed, slipping on the steep track. Indeed, quite half the descent she accomplished sitting down. But at last she felt sand beneath her feet, and she stood up, peering about her and trying to see across the beach. A second or two later there came the sound of oars being moved quietly in rowlocks, and then the scrape of a keel on the beach. Charlotte could see nothing, but guessed that a rowing-boat must have come in from the smugglers' ship out in the cove.

She stood for some moments, undecided what to do, then she heard other footsteps coming down the cliff path above her. Clearly, if she was to get Tom's message to Mr. Tregelles, she would either have to give it to someone to pass on, or take it aboard the smugglers' boat herself. It did not take her long to decide to follow the latter course.

She began walking down the beach to the water-line. Behind her she heard the footsteps catching up with her, and Charlotte was aware that her heart was beating with uncomfortable speed. The shape of a small rowing-boat loomed up, and Charlotte thought of what she would say to the man at the oars.

But when she reached the little craft, the man only grunted a greeting and bade her get in quickly; and so

Charlotte clambered aboard, and was soon followed by the man she had heard coming down the cliff face.

Without anything further being said, the oarsman began to row; the beach soon disappeared into the mist, and Charlotte glanced cautiously at her companions in the boat. But it was too dark to see their faces, and she concentrated on the regular sound of the oars dipping into the water.

It was not long before a huge shape rose out of the sea ahead of them, and in a minute or two they were stopped alongside. The other passengers stood up, and Charlotte watched as the first man grasped what appeared to be a rope, and swarmed up it to the deck above. The second man followed the first, and now Charlotte also rose, wondering how she could possibly manage to climb the rope, and wearing Tom's boots into the bargain — which were slightly too large. What should she do if one of the boots — or both of them — fell off?

The man at the oars muttered something about making haste, and Charlotte held out her hand to take the rope. To her relief she saw that it was, in fact, a rope ladder, and thankfully she scrambled up it as fast as she could. She felt some alarm when she heard the rowing-boat moving away again at once, but thought that it must have gone back to the shore to bring out some more smugglers. She would give Mr. Tregelles the message, then climb down the ladder and get herself taken back to shore, on the boat's next trip.

When Charlotte's face was level with the deck, she looked about very cautiously, fearful of what she might encounter. She felt some relief when at first she saw and heard no-one, and she clambered onto the deck, and stood still, wondering where she could find Mr. Tregelles. She crept forward a pace or two, and almost at once found herself seized roughly. Only by the very greatest self-control did Charlotte manage not to emit a maidenly shriek.

'Where're 'ee goin', boy?' a rough voice demanded quietly.

'I be lookin' for Mr. Tregelles,' Charlotte managed to whisper, attempting a local accent.

The man made a disapproving noise. ' 'Ee'll find un below.'

Then Charlotte was released, and the man pushed past her.

The girl looked about her, and thought that she felt a breath of wind on her cheek. She looked upwards, and it seemed to her that the mist was rising swiftly. She looked towards the shore, and she thought she could make out the shape of the cliffs.

A moment later she became conscious of noises on board. Where all had been quiet before, now there were unknown noises. Charlotte made her way forward a pace or two where she thought she must find the way down to the cabin, and was startled by a low whistle, which was immediately followed by the noise of metal rattling against wood. Now in the dim light she could make out figures hauling on something; the timbers of the boat creaked, and the sound of the water lapping against the boat's side seemed to change. There came a flapping noise next, and a shudder seemed to run through the boat; the wind seemed to blow more strongly, and it took no more than another three moments for Charlotte to realise that the boat was under way.

She looked about her in consternation. She was trapped on the smugglers' boat, and it was taking her to France! She wanted to shout out 'Stop! I must get off!' But her voice would not leave her throat. Gripping the boat-rail, she stared down at the water which was now rushing by, judging by the strip of white she could see below her.

She must have reached Melyn Cove much later than she had thought. And in any case she need not have come, for Mr. Tregelles had set out without waiting for Tom. She must let him know at once that she was on board, and then she could get off and go back to the vicarage, and — Charlotte's hair almost rose on end as she thought of the scrape she now found herself in. The little rowing-boat was already returned to shore, and there was no means for her to return anyway! And she could hardly think that the smugglers would agree to turn about so that she could get back to land!

Even so, she had better let Mr. Tregelles know at once that she was there. Charlotte took a few more paces forward. There was just enough light for her to see men still making fast the sail-lines, and she clung to the rail as the boat keeled over to one side. She would ask one of the sailors how she should get to Mr. Tregelles . . .

At that moment, another idea came to her. There was no point now in her telling Mr. Tregelles that Tom would not be coming, and therefore — she might keep secret from the marquis that she was aboard dressed in men's clothes. It was not something of which he would approve, she felt sure, and . . . well, she did wish to retain the Frenchman's approval. Her imagination presented all too vivid a picture of how the marquis would look when he saw her in breeches, and it was the work of but a moment to decide that she must remain hidden till they were returned to England. Somehow then, she would slip off the boat and return to the vicarage and say nothing at all — no matter how her aunt Radley stormed at her.

So she felt about her cautiously, her eyes fixed on the sailors, and it was not long before she came to what felt like a little niche in which was lying a pile of folded canvas. The cloth was stiff and heavy, but somehow Charlotte managed to make a sort of nest into which she crept, and she crouched there, tense and still, ready to pull a loose piece of canvas over her head if anyone came by her.

4

It was cold and cramped in the corner into which Charlotte had crept. At first excitement had kept her warm, but soon her discomfort was such that she could not put it out of her mind. The folds of canvas lay heavily on her legs, so that it was an effort to move them to ease the stiffness which soon grew in them. There was no moonlight at all, but the stars which she could just see shone down very brightly; and though the boat seemed unnaturally quiet, apart from the sound of the wind in the sails, and the sea rushing by below her, Charlotte was constantly alert, ready to burrow into her hiding-place if footsteps should approach her. Very occasionally she heard a muffled voice, but it was gone almost as soon as she had heard it; and Charlotte was overwhelmed by an eerie sensation, almost as if she were quite alone on the boat.

At the beginning she had managed to draw some comfort from the fact that the wind was behind them, and that they were speeding along. The sooner they got to France, the sooner they would be back at Melyn Cove, and Charlotte herself safe in bed at St. Bride's vicarage.

But as they left the coast behind them, and proceeded through open water, the rolling of the boat grew very pronounced; Charlotte felt more and more uneasy, and soon — decidedly unwell. It was not long before the queasiness of her stomach had over-come all other sensations, and Charlotte could only lie there, feeling that death would be preferable, and quite unable to restrain a low moan from time to time.

It was one such expression of her anguish that was eventually to prove her undoing. One moment, she had been sitting with her eyes closed, and her knees drawn up, her hands holding her stomach, thinking how exceedingly ill she felt; the next moment, her arm had been seized, she had been pulled from her hiding-place in no gentle fashion, and a rough voice was demanding what she did.

Charlotte could only stand blinking for some seconds, feeling more unwell than ever, and quite unable to gather her thoughts sufficiently to make any answer. The man shook her arm again, demanding now to know who she was.

' 'Ee knows what us dooes wi' stowaways, don' 'ee?' he hissed. 'Us claps they in irons!'

'I — I am going to be ill!' Charlotte gasped urgently.

The man hauled her ungently to the rail, and Charlotte leant over it, and immediately lost her dinner. She straightened after some moments, feeling much better, and with her free hand sought a kerchief in one of her pockets. She wiped her face with a shaking hand.

97

'Well, do 'ee speak up now,' the man growled, shaking her arm once more.

'I — I wish to speak with Mr. Tregelles!' Charlotte quavered with what dignity she could muster, fear now succeeding her queasiness.

'Oh, 'ee do, do 'ee? Well, 'ee'd best see the cap'n,' the man returned, but a little uncertainly now.

Charlotte sensed this, and managed a little more firmly, 'I — I hardly think Mr. Tregelles would care to find me in irons!'

The man peered down at her, and though Charlotte could not see his expression, she felt his indecision more strongly than ever. Then abruptly he turned on his heel, and began to haul her after him, muttering something which Charlotte could not catch. After a few paces along the deck, they went down a short companionway, the man knocked at a door, and in answer to a brisk 'Come in,' her captor opened the door and pulled her into the cabin.

Charlotte blinked as the light from a

three-branched candlestick met her eyes.

'This lad says as 'e's a message for 'ee, sir,' the man said, addressing Richard Tregelles, who was seated at a table. The man gave Charlotte a push forward. 'I found 'un stowed away aft.'

Richard Tregelles turned in his chair and stared at Charlotte. 'Well, what is it, boy?' he asked curtly.

'I — I have a message for 'ee sir,' Charlotte said as calmly as she could, again attempting a local accent. 'From — from Tom Radley.'

Mr. Tregelles stared at her for a moment; then a puzzled expression came to his face. He jumped to his feet, seized the candlestick and came close to her, holding the branch up so that the light fell full on her face.

Then he turned to Charlotte's captor. 'It's quite all right. You can leave the — boy here. I know him.'

'If 'ee's sure, sir.'

'Yes, I am.'

The man grunted, turned on his heel

and went out, closing the door behind him.

Charlotte stared back at Mr. Tregelles, her heart thumping uncomfortably, but endeavouring to look unconcerned. After all, it was not her fault that she was on the boat. Certainly she had no wish to be there. She glanced past Richard Tregelles into the cabin, and saw that the marquis was not there. She wondered where he was.

'Well, Miss Charlotte Radley!' Mr. Tregelles said in a whisper. 'What do you think you're doing here?'

'I have no wish to be here, sir, I assure you!' Charlotte returned in a cross whisper. 'But I came with a message from my cousin Tom. You set out before I could deliver it!' she ended accusingly.

'I am very sorry for that!' Mr. Tregelles returned, with an odious smile. He looked Charlotte up and down, taking in her breeches and boots. 'But I must say, you make a delightful youth, ma'am!'

Charlotte flushed with annoyance and mortification. 'Do not you wish to know my message?' she demanded tartly.

'Ah, yes, Radley! I wondered what had happened to him.'

Mr. Tregelles' tone angered Charlotte still further. She had always thought Mr. Tregelles a rather disagreeable creature, but now — ! 'Only wondered!' she remarked acidly. 'And there was my poor cousin, on his bed of pain, worrying himself into a fever that he would let you down, and to comfort him, I promised to bring you a message, which clearly you do not care in the least to hear, and I might well have saved myself a good deal of discomfort — and — and danger!'

Mr. Tregelles at once looked contrite. 'I am so sorry, Miss Charlotte,' he whispered. 'Pray come and sit down, and give me the message.'

Charlotte allowed herself to be led to the table in the centre of the room, and seated in one of the chairs there.

'Well, ma'am?' Mr. Tregelles smiled encouragingly, as he seated himself opposite her.

'My cousin much regrets that — that he was unable to join you. But — his leg is broken. He went out last night, and you remember what a night it was! His horse slipped, and Tom was thrown and his leg damaged. Mr. Maker, the surgeon came to set it, and says that Tom should do very well.'

'A broken leg, you say!' Mr. Tregelles looked very concerned.

'My cousin was so anxious that you should know that he could not join you . . . '

'I must thank you very much, ma'am, for undertaking to bring the message. It can not have been at all pleasant, coming out in the mist. I trust you had — no untoward adventures on your way to Melyn Cove.'

Charlotte looked at Mr. Tregelles suspiciously, but she could see no sign of amusement in his face.

'Apart from encountering a creature

who was exceedingly foxed, sir, the untoward adventure began only when I reached the cove.'

'Ah, yes, indeed!' Now Mr. Tregelles' eyes did twinkle, and Charlotte was quite unable to repress a smile. 'But,' Mr. Tregelles continued after a moment, his brow darkening, 'Tom Radley had no business to put you in such a situation! He must have been mad to ask you to venture out on such an errand!' Mr. Tregelles paused, and looked at Charlotte with a worried expression on his countenance. 'I am afraid it was after he had seen me that Tom had his accident. He had come to Pentallack to find out the final details . . . '

'He was to help you in the rescue of Mademoiselle MontSauvage?'

Mr. Tregelles nodded, and gazed at Charlotte again. 'Oh, Miss Charlotte,' he murmured after some moments, 'what on earth am I going to do with you now?'

'I am quite capable of looking after

myself, sir!' Charlotte muttered stiffly.

'No doubt!' Mr. Tregelles returned with a twinkle in his eye. 'But I must point out to you, ma'am, that — we are on a smugglers' boat, making for France — a country with which Britain is at war! We are hardly well — prepared to look after a female!'

'I collect that you expect to bring back Mademoiselle MontSauvage, sir! What a Frenchwoman may endure, so, I should hope, can I!'

Mr. Tregelles regarded her now with frank admiration. 'Your cousin, Tom Radley, is in the right, ma'am! You are a female of remarkable courage!' And he picked up Charlotte's hand which was resting upon the table between them, and carried it to his lips. Charlotte blushed, and felt oddly pleased.

'It will be some time before we reach the French coast, ma'am,' Mr. Tregelles continued after a moment. 'Even with this wind, we shall be some hours. You will be quite safe in here till then. I would offer you the sleeping cabin, ma'am, but — it is already occupied.'

'Oh?'

'Yes. MontSauvage is there. He is no sailor. I — I could turn him out for you,' he added after a moment.

'Oh, no! I thank you. I am quite well — now!' Charlotte smiled at the recollection of how ill she had felt. 'I — I wondered where the marquis was. But I remember to have heard before that — he was not happy at sea.'

'Will you take some wine, ma'am?'

'No, I thank you, sir.'

A short silence descended then, during which Mr. Tregelles continued to regard Charlotte, while she herself gazed round the cabin. She had never been on a boat before, and was impressed by the tidiness of everything. Apart from Mr. Tregelles' cape on the door, and his book open upon the table, there was nothing about the cabin at all. Charlotte guessed that whatever was for use was stowed in the chest she could see in one corner, or in the big cupboard on one wall. She wondered where the wine was kept.

She caught Mr. Tregelles' eye, and the silence suddenly seemed oppressive.

'W — what was my cousin to do when you got to France?' she asked for the sake of saying something.

'He was to be a look-out.'

'I see. And what will you do now?'

'I dare say that we shall manage without.'

A daring thought came into Charlotte's head. Had not Tom called her errand to Mr. Tregelles an adventure? Why should not it now become a much greater one? She said very nonchalantly, regarding Mr. Tregelles from under her eyelids, 'Mr. Tregelles, why do not *I* take my cousin's place?'

'You must be mad, ma'am!' was Mr. Tregelles' gallant reply.

His tone irritated Charlotte. 'Not at all, sir!' she retorted. 'And I warrant I speak better French than does my cousin Tom!'

'We had not thought that any French would be necessary!'

Charlotte continued to regard Mr. Tregelles from under her lowered eyelids, the idea of actually *doing* something to rescue Mademoiselle MontSauvage growing more and more appealing. Besides, if Mr. Tregelles' plans had to be altered because of Tom's absence, it seemed only sensible that she should do what he should have done. And it was true, she *did* speak French very well.

'Do I collect that — my cousin's absence is very material, sir?' she asked innocently, after some moments.

'I would have felt rather happier with someone to watch for us,' Mr. Tregelles answered a little hesitatingly. 'But — we must manage without,' he ended very firmly. 'Tom's leg should mend well, you say?'

'So Mr. Maker said. What exactly was it that Tom should have done?' she pursued. 'I am only interested,' she added, when Mr. Tregelles seemed to hesitate to answer.

'Tom was to wait near the castle

gates, and give notice of the approach of any soldiers.'

'Oh, really? And how was he to do it?'

'He was to hoot like an owl.'

Charlotte grinned. 'I can see that Tom would have enjoyed it. But — how came he to be of your party? I had thought Tom — I mean — one of your own friends . . . ?'

'When MontSauvage first came to England, Tom begged to be taken if we should ever return for Mademoiselle MontSauvage. He mentioned it at my parents' ball — as soon as he knew what had been done for MontSauvage.'

'Did he indeed!' Charlotte remarked, remembering how little-pleased Tom had looked when she and Kitty had come to him and Kitty had asked her brother to present Mr. Tregelles to Charlotte. 'Well, I am sure he is very upset not to be here now.'

A silence ensued again.

'Miss Charlotte,' Mr. Tregelles said a little later, 'there is one thing that has always puzzled me . . . '

'Indeed, sir?'

'Yes. And when you first came to the cabin, dressed as you are, I was reminded of it.'

'Really?' Charlotte murmured, being pretty certain what was to come.

'Yes,' Mr. Tregelles said, with an admirably straight face; 'in fact, I thought you looked remarkably familiar . . .'

'I can not think what you mean, sir!' Charlotte attempted to sound totally innocent. But she saw at once that it would not do.

'No? Well, I will tell you what puzzles me, ma'am. That evening, when we brought in MontSauvage — the same evening, you recall, that you and Miss Kitty had your unfortunate encounter with the smugglers — at Melyn Cove, I believe — '

Charlotte watched Mr. Tregelles' face carefully, trying to think how she should answer. She made no reply now, but left him to speak.

' . . . when we were coming up the cliffs, one of our men came upon two young gentlemen . . . '

'Oh, really?'

'And — I have always had the greatest curiosity to know — exactly what they were doing there.' Mr. Tregelles eyed Charlotte curiously. 'You see, ma'am, it seemed to me so — extraordinary, that they should be at that very spot — at that very time — '

'It was indeed very odd!'

'And then — you and Miss Kitty also met smugglers that night!'

'Yes.'

'I wondered, at first, if we had been betrayed.'

'Oh, no!'

'No?' Mr. Tregelles said, looking at Charlotte very hard.

'I am sure — it was but a coincidence, sir.'

'I am very glad for that!' Mr. Tregelles smiled. 'But — I can not help wondering — why the youths were there.'

'Perhaps,' Charlotte said slowly after a moment, 'perhaps — they had been to the fair at Trevannock.'

'Ah, yes! I had forgot that!' Mr. Tregelles said quietly.

The two looked at each other in silence for some moments. Charlotte, surprised by Mr. Tregelles' delicacy in not asking his question straight out, had now admitted, as plainly as if she had said it, that she and Kitty and the two unknown young men were one and the same pair. But she had, thereby, only confirmed Mr. Tregelles' suspicions. Having conceded so much, she must attempt to ensure that the secret went no further.

'I dare say you have told very few people that — that you and M. MontSauvage are on this boat tonight, sir?' She had, after all, a secret in exchange.

'We have told no-one, ma'am!' Mr. Tregelles exclaimed. 'Apart from Tom, of course.'

'That is what I thought,' Charlotte

111

nodded. 'It is always best to keep a secret known to as few as possible — if you wish it to remain a secret, that is.'

'My own sentiments exactly, ma'am.'

Charlotte said no more, but gave Mr. Tregelles a meaning look.

After a moment, he said, 'I dare say that — the young men we met at Melyn Cove — might well prefer their presence there not to be known to too many.'

'I dare say. And — I expect they could see very little.'

'There was no moon that night.'

'They should have had — a lookout,' Charlotte smiled.

'Yes. It might have been very useful.'

'Just as you would wish to have one tonight, sir. There is one at your service.'

'I would not dream of taking advantage of the offer, ma'am.'

'It does not seem — a very difficult job — '

'On *no* account, ma'am.'

Gracefully, Charlotte let the subject

drop for the time, satisfied now that Mr. Tregelles would tell no-one of her and Kitty's escapade. She could only hope he had not mentioned his suspicions already, but of course she could not ask Mr. Tregelles about that — though she thought the marquis remained in ignorance.

The wind continued strong behind them all the way across the Channel. They had the good fortune to meet no other ships on the voyage, and they reached the French coast quite a while earlier than their best expectations. All this time, Charlotte had seen nothing of the marquis. She would have been a good deal happier if she could have been assured that he would have been glad to see her when he did eventually emerge from the cabin, but everything that she knew of him could only strengthen her doubts on the matter. She almost wished that they might never reach France, so that the evil hour might be delayed for ever.

But when Tregarth came down to say

that they would be at the French coast within twenty minutes, Charlotte prepared herself to meet the marquis's disapproval. There was, after all, nothing she could do to avoid it, and she must carry it off as best she could.

Richard Tregelles now began to worry as to what should become of Charlotte while he and the marquis were away.

'If I were with you, sir . . . '

'On no account, ma'am. But neither can I like to leave you here.' And he gazed at her in some perplexity.

When the boat was stationary once more, Charlotte was still not certain if he had made up his mind as to what she should do while he and the marquis were away.

She happened to be in the shadows when the Marquis de MontSauvage emerged at last from the sleeping cabin. He did not see her at first, and spoke in rapid French to Richard Tregelles. Then the marquis made for the door, but just as he was about to pass through it, he turned round and spoke again to the Englishman. In so doing he caught sight of Charlotte.

'Are you come in place of Radley?' he demanded at once. 'Why did not you tell me, Dick, that all was well?'

'Yes, I am!' Charlotte answered at once in a very firm voice.

'No, he has but brought — '

But before Richard Tregelles could finish his sentence, Tregarth appeared in the cabin door once more, and urged them to hurry onto the deck.

'Come, then; let us not waste time!' the marquis declared, and promptly turned and followed the captain up the companionway.

Greatly excited, Charlotte crossed the cabin to follow the marquis. Richard Tregelles put out his hand and stopped her. 'And where are you going?'

'With you, of course!'

'Never, ma'am!'

'It is plain that I can not stay here,' Charlotte retorted. 'You know it, yourself. What! You would not leave me alone with Tregarth and his men! I should be a deal safer with you and M. MontSauvage.'

At that moment, Tregarth appeared again. 'Do come, sir. We may stay here only a few moments, and the boat is waiting to take you in!'

'Go on then — boy!' Richard Tregelles muttered, in a voice in which exasperation was uppermost.

Charlotte did as she was bid, and hurried up the companionway and onto the deck. She could see the cliffs of France ahead, but had no time to look about her, for Tregarth told her to move aft, and hurriedly she did so, and was in time to see the marquis climbing over the rail, and down the rope ladder.

After the smallest hesitation, Charlotte followed, still amazed that she had escaped recognition by the marquis. But then, he had hardly stopped to look at her.

She managed to get down the rope

ladder reasonably speedily, but almost fell from the ladder into the rowing-boat, and the marquis caught her wrist and steadied her.

'Be careful!' he muttered impatiently. 'I have no wish to fall into the water!'

Charlotte sat down in the little boat as far away from the marquis as she could. Richard Tregelles followed her down the ladder, then Tregarth, and in a moment, the rowing-boat was pulling away from the bigger vessel. Charlotte looked fearfully towards the coast, realising for the first time exactly what it was she had let herself in for, and thinking with a good deal of longing, of her safe, warm bed in St. Bride's vicarage. She shivered as the cold wind blew over them, and in a moment, she felt Richard Tregelles' hand warm on her arm. She felt comforted by the gesture, and smiled at him gratefully in the darkness.

Now Charlotte did strain her eyes ahead to the coast, wondering if they would land unseen, or if they were moving into an ambush. Tregarth began speaking in a low voice to Richard Tregelles, and Charlotte glanced surreptitiously at the marquis. It was far too dark to see his expression, but she was aware that he too was staring at the nearing cliffs.

It was not long before the rowing-boat scraped onto the shingle. The marquis was out first, followed by Tregarth. When Charlotte stood up, Richard held her arm to steady her. She jumped down onto the beach, squelching in the wet sand.

There was a brief, hurried consultation between the three men.

'We must be away by three o'clock, sir,' Tregarth whispered with finality.

'I know. And you will not wait. We shall be ready for you.'

'Good.' Tregarth got into the boat again, which at once began pulling back to the vessel standing off shore.

'And now,' Richard Tregelles said in a low voice to Charlotte, 'we must find somewhere to hide you safely.'

'I am coming with you!' Charlotte returned.

'This is no lively scheme, Miss Radley!' Richard whispered hotly. 'If we are caught, we might well end up on the guillotine!'

'But I should be far more frightened to remain here!'

'If you stay on this beach you will be here when the boat comes back, and there will be no doubt of your getting back to England. The rowing-boat will come in and — '

The marquis came up to them then. 'Come, Dick, why do you delay? Does not this fellow know what to do?'

'I shall manage very well if you will only show me the place!' Charlotte whispered.

'Have you forgot it already?' the marquis demanded impatiently. 'Why did not Radley — ?'

'I have not forgotten — !' Charlotte began.

But the marquis broke in. 'We have little enough time as it is if we are to catch the tide back to England. Do let us get on, Dick!'

And the marquis began to walk up the beach, his boots crunching on the small stones.

'You see I can not possibly remain here!' Charlotte whispered. 'It is a ridiculous thought.'

And she too turned and began marching after the marquis. Richard's footsteps started after her. Very quickly he caught up with her, and took her arm. 'Do you think you are being fair, ma'am?' he asked quietly. 'Do you think I want the responsibility of another female at this time? I am convinced from what I have heard of her that Mademoiselle MontSauvage will be more than enough to manage!'

Charlotte had not looked at the matter in this light, and at once felt abashed, and even sorry for Mr. Tregelles. 'I am very sorry,' she whispered. 'But — I did not mean to come! But now that I am here, I promise to do exactly what you tell me, if only you will not leave me on this beach, where I truly think that I might die of fright. And — and you did say that it would be easier if Tom were with you to keep watch!'

Richard made no reply for some minutes, but the hand that held her arm grasped her more gently, and he helped her over the rocky places. They could hear the marquis ahead, clambering quietly over the rocks.

'You had better tell me what I must do,' Charlotte whispered in a low voice.

'I do not approve at all, ma'am,' Richard Tregelles returned. 'But since you are here — and if you promise to obey — '

'Oh, I will! I will!'

Richard then explained in detail exactly what Tom Radley's part in the rescue was to have been: how he was to wait hidden near the gates of the castle, ready to give warning if anyone should enter while he, Tregelles, and the marquis were inside. If soldiers, or anyone else, entered the castle gate, the agreed warning was to be given, so that the little party might leave the castle by another way.

'The warning signal is three owl hoots, followed by another group of three. Then a pause, and repeat the call. You repeat the whole again after two minutes. The castle is not far from the road; you need not fear you will not be heard if you give a loud call. Do you think you can do it?'

'I do not see why not!'

'We will try it when we are inland. I do not think there are many owls to be found on a beach!'

'Have we far to go?'

'A little less than three miles, I believe. It took me about an hour to walk there before.'

Charlotte thought thankfully that her cousin's boots were reasonably comfortable with the thick hose she had found.

The marquis seemed to have the eyes of a cat. He moved forward unhesitatingly, with Richard and Charlotte behind. Richard continued to grasp Charlotte's arm, steadying her over the awkward places. As they began to climb, any talking between them ceased. The cliff was steep as was the cliff at Melyn Cove, and whereas Charlotte had come down the one, sitting down for most of the way, here on this French cliff she came up it practically upon her knees.

Once at the top, they struck off across fields, and when they were well inland, Richard made them pause to rest for some minutes, and so that Charlotte might practise her owl hoots. She accomplished the signal in exemplary fashion, and Richard congratulated her, though all the while the marquis was impatient to continue their journey.

He brought them round to his château, which was a little outside the village, skirting it by continuing through fields, and not along the track which they eventually came upon. The starlight gave more than sufficient light for them to see their way plainly; but also for them to be seen. Richard made them creep along in the shade of hedges, and it was a little over an hour before they stood under the castle wall. Charlotte was quite breathless when they arrived, but did her best to hide it, not wishing Richard to consider her an even greater burden than he did already.

The hiding-place chosen for Charlotte was a ditch which ran across the field in front of the château gates. Here she had a good view of the entrance to the castle, and also of the lane leading from the village. At the castle gates this track divided to skirt the castle walls on both sides.

'If anyone enters the gate — anyone at all — a single person or more, soldiers or peasants, give the call,' Richard said.

'Six owl hoots, then a pause, then six more,' Charlotte answered confidently. 'Then repeat it after two minutes.'

The marquis nodded. 'Good. It will

give us some small chance of getting away before anyone arrives there. If it is necessary, we shall leave by the cellar passage. When we are safely out of the castle grounds, we will give the signal, which you will return, and so we may find you. You understand, Monsieur?'

'Yes.'

'And if we should be captured,' Richard said hastily, 'if you hear nothing from us, you are to leave here as soon as the village clock strikes two o'clock. Is that understood?'

'Yes,' whispered Charlotte.

'You are on no account to try to find us, or enter the castle grounds; is that clear?' Richard continued.

Charlotte nodded.

'Two o'clock will be short time enough for you to reach the shore, but you should be able to get down the cliff faster then we came up,' Richard said, with what Charlotte thought was a smile in his voice. 'You promise to leave at once?'

'Yes,' Charlotte whispered again.

'And if my sister is — is no longer at the château, we will be returned within the half hour,' the marquis added. 'Come, Dick.'

Suddenly Richard put his other hand on Charlotte's arm. He had retained his hold with his other hand all this time. 'Take care of yourself. And keep down. Do not let yourself be seen.'

'I shall be all right!' Charlotte answered more stoutly than she felt. 'Good luck! I look forward to meeting Mademoiselle soon.'

The marquis moved off. Richard gave her arm a little squeeze, before he too turned and slipped away, leaving Charlotte alone. The girl crouched down, half protected by the ditch, half by a clump of bushes, listening and watching intently. Almost at once the sound of the men's footsteps died away, and she could not see so much as a shadow to tell her where they were. Then there were only the usual rustling sounds of the night.

With swiftly beating heart, Charlotte

settled down to her watch, part of her wishing that the marquis might know what she was doing for his and his sister's sake, part of her piqued because he so obviously had not had the least idea as to her identity.

And another part of her made her smile a little, as she thought of Richard Tregelles' obvious concern for her.

5

At first Charlotte's greatest fear was that she would be discovered. During the first minutes she was there, no-one moved on any of the tracks. Then a horseman trotted out of the village, and Charlotte watched, holding her breath, ready to let out the signal. But the man turned to the left at the castle gates, and Charlotte relaxed.

Next she hard raucous singing, and shouting in rough voices from the direction of the village, which lay only a few hundred yards behind her. The shouting seemed to her to grow angrier, then there was a silence, followed by laughter, and the singing began again, then gradually faded away.

After that a creaking cart came from the right of the castle, and turned left into the road to the village.

It seemed to Charlotte that there

were a great many people abroad in the little French village, and she wondered if St. Bride's was as busy after dark. This made her think of what might be happening at the vicarage now; had Kitty been able to keep her absence hidden, or was she so worried that all had been revealed? Surely, if that had occurred, Tom would guess what had happened and . . . well, Aunt Radley would undoubtedly be exceedingly angry, but — it was, after all, hardly Charlotte's fault . . . and if she explained how very frightened she had been — and was — at this very moment!

To Charlotte's appalled ears came the sound of something moving across the field towards her. At first she could not imagine what it was: she could hear panting, and the sound of bounding across the grass; the next moment, what appeared to be a huge dog was attempting to lick her face, and uttering happy little cries.

'Go away! Be quiet! Leave me alone!'

Charlotte hissed, fending off the creature's long pink tongue, which seemed intent on giving her countenance a thorough wash. The dog took absolutely no notice, but continued to poke at her with his muzzle, and Charlotte, who was really very fond of dogs, gave it a pat or two to try to calm it. After all, it was quite friendly. It would have been — would *be* — a very different kettle of fish if it grew — unfriendly!

'Good dog! Now do be quiet! Just sit quietly. But — I really would like it much better if only you would go home!'

The dog merely raised one paw, and let it fall heavily on Charlotte's arm.

She was gazing somewhat despairingly at the animal, and patting it mechanically when the sound of several pairs of feet moving up the road from the village came to her ears. At once she crouched down in the ditch, peering over the top, watching the dark shadows of the men. Her hand remained resting on the dog's head, and to her relief, the animal remained as still and quiet as herself.

Charlotte saw the men move to the end of the track and pause by the castle gate. There they stopped, and stayed for what seemed to the watching girl at least a quarter of an hour. She could hear the sound of their voices, but not their words, and she was sure that at any moment now she would have to give the signal.

But to her great relief, the men divided into two groups, one turning off to the left, the other to the right. Charlotte let out a sigh of relief, and eased her tense limbs. She felt the dog relax also, and patted him again.

'Good boy. Very good boy!'

It seemed to Charlotte that the dog was pleased with her praise.

It was shortly after this that she heard the village clock strike one. It was about now that her concern for her own safety changed to anxiety as to what was going on in the castle. The marquis and Mr. Tregelles had been gone near an hour now; clearly Mademoiselle MontSauvage was in the castle or they would surely be returned by now — but what could be holding them up? Charlotte could imagine no reason for the delay, until the uncomfortable thought came to her that perhaps the wretched young woman was again refusing to escape with her brother!

By now Charlotte was sadly stiff, and longed to stretch her cramped legs. Fearfully, she looked and listened for sounds of movement, but there was nothing. Very gingerly, therefore, Charlotte stood up. The dog was up at once, clearly expecting that they were to move on, and he dashed off happily. But when Charlotte did not follow him, he ran back to see what was detaining her. Keeping to the shadow of the bushes, the girl walked about for a few paces, the dog watching her, clearly puzzled.

Charlotte's agitation was increasing by the minute. As time went by and there was still no sign of the others, she began to wonder if they would ever return, and if it would be necessary for her to make her way back to the beach alone. She must certainly leave the moment she heard two o'clock strike, but even then, she might well miss her way, and be too late to catch the boat, and then be stranded in France!

The more she thought about her situation, the less she could like it, and she was almost grateful for the dog's presence in her vigil. At least she was not quite alone.

It was then that she heard the sounds of marching feet. This group was different from the other footsteps she had heard: it was more regular — and there seemed to be more men in the group. Charlotte crouched down again, and peered between the lowest leaves of the bushes. To her horror she was immediately certain that what she was looking at was a group of soldiers! Althought there was no moon, the starlight was strong enough to glint off the pikes that the men were carrying over their shoulders.

Charlotte watched, at first almost numb with fear. The tread of the men moved on inexorably, nearer, nearer to the castle gates. Charlotte's heart hammered against her ribs, and her mouth felt dry. Would they turn off to right or left at the gates — or would they continue past them to the castle!

At the junction, the men paused; then an order was given, and the group moved forward. Charlotte's worst fears were realised when she saw the men march straight ahead.

At once she got to her feet and prepared to let out a hoot like an owl. At her first attempt, no sound at all issued from her lips. She took a deep breath and tried again.

'To — whooo! To — whooo! To — whooo!' she managed to call, albeit in a wavering fashion, repeating it after a moment.

She called again! 'To — whoooo! To — whoooo! To — whooooooooo!' six times. Her voice was stronger now. She began counting off the one hundred and twenty seconds before she should repeat the call.

She saw the dog watching her, clearly not comprehending, but mercifully standing still.

'One hundred and nineteen,' she muttered under her breath; 'One hundred and twenty. To — whooooo! To — whooooo!'

The dog began growling low down in his throat, and it was all Charlotte could do to get out the last hoot. Fearfully she turned to look at the dog. Its body was rigid, and the low rumbling continued in its throat. She turned her head a little more, and drew in another breath to repeat the agreed signal. She was certain someone was just going to spring upon her, and she must complete the alarm before she was captured.

'To — wh-oo — oo — oo — ' she called frantically.

'Psst!' a voice close at hand hissed. 'It's all right! We are here!'

Charlotte spun round and saw

Richard Tregelles at her elbow. The dog was still growling in its throat. Without thinking, Charlotte was about to throw herself unblushingly into Mr. Tregelles' arms, so thankful was she to see him, when swiftly, he laid his hand on her own arm. 'Come, — er — Charles,' he said warningly. 'We have no time to lose!'

'Some soldiers have just passed through the gates!' Charlotte gasped.

'I know. We saw them.'

'Oh, thank God you are come! I was so frightened that you had all been captured!'

'No. We are all three of us safe. But we must leave at once!'

'But where are — ?'

'Just beside the road into the village.'

'But surely we are not — !'

At that moment, the cracked bell of the village clock sounded out two o'clock in the morning.

'It will be safer, we think. They will hardly expect us to pass through an inhabited area.'

Richard began to draw Charlotte down the field, keeping in the shadow of the bushes bordering the hedge as far as possible. The dog followed at a little distance.

'I did not see you come out of the castle gates!' Charlotte whispered.

'We came out another way — fortunately.'

In a few more moments Charlotte made out two figures ahead. She heard the dog growl again.

'Where did this creature come from?' demanded Richard in a low voice.

'He just appeared. I think he is lonely.'

'Well, I would be a deal happier without him!'

'He may return home when we reach the village.'

They reached the waiting figures, and Richard said, 'This is — Charles Radley, Mademoiselle.'

One of the figures held out her hand, and Charlotte, greatly taken aback, only just stopped herself curtsying, and managed to take the hand and bend over it, mumbling 'Mademoiselle!' as she did so.

'We must make haste,' the marquis whispered, 'or we will miss the boat!'

'Is it not shorter through the village?'

'Yes. But we must take care not to make the least sound.'

The four of them crept along the edge of the ditch, till it crossed a little path which ran to join the main road through the village. At first, the marquis and his sister led the way, but when the road was reached, Charlotte found herself walking behind with the marquis, while Richard and Mademoiselle MontSauvage went first. Thankfully, the dog seemed to have disappeared.

As they passed the first houses, all was quiet, and it seemed that the little village was sleeping peacefully at last. But when they had reached the village square, suddenly, a few houses ahead of them, a door opened, men's voices were heard, and three figures appeared on the roadway. There was some laughter, and then the door was shut, and the three men began to walk in the direction of the quartette.

Charlotte watched terrified. These men also looked like soldiers, and it would be too terrible if they were all caught by them now! When the door had first opened, the four of them had sunk back into the deep shadow of a wall. Now Charlotte felt herself being pulled through a doorway by the marquis, and in another moment she was crouching behind a heap of straw beside him. She did not see Mademoiselle MontSauvage and Mr. Tregelles enter, but now she, heard quite clearly a shout from the lane, and the sound of hurrying feet. She guessed that they must be in a barn, judging by the straw and the smell of animals, and cautiously Charlotte looked about her. The marquis was only a dark blur crouching beside her.

Across the barn floor the open doorway was a pale rectangle. In a moment figures appeared in it, shouting in French, demanding to know who was there. As she peered across the space with frightened eyes, Charlotte thought she could make out the shape of a musket in the hands of one of the men.

She knew she was right a second later when the man raised it as if to fire.

Then a woman's giggle came from somewhere in the barn, and a young girl's voice called out to the man, begging him not to shoot. But it was not at all the sort of voice Charlotte would have expected to hear from the young marquise: it sounded decidedly foxed, and the girl hiccoughed once or twice as she called to the men, and giggled again.

The men laughed now, and shouted back something which Charlotte did not understand.

She felt the marquis beside her stiffen, and she thought he muttered something under his breath. Charlotte crouched low behind the straw, peering across the barn to where the girl's voice came from. Surely it must be Mademoiselle MontSauvage! There could not be anyone else hiding in the barn!

The marquis gave a smothered gasp, and then, to Charlotte's astonishment, she saw Richard Tregelles come out of the shadow, leading the French girl by the hand. He was without his coat, and his shirt was half-unbuttoned, and he was laughing also. At least, that was what Charlotte thought she saw in the dimness. What she could make no mistake about was what happened next.

Quite distinctly, Charlotte saw him catch hold of Mademoiselle MontSauvage, then he shouted something to the three men, who began to laugh uproariously, then he pulled the young Frenchwoman down onto a pile of straw just by them, and began to kiss her unrestrainedly.

More giggles issued from Mademoiselle MontSauvage, and the three men by the door laughed and shouted several things which it was lucky for Charlotte's modesty that she could not understand. Richard Tregelles shouted back in a similar vein, and then at last the three men left the barn and reeled off into the night.

Charlotte and the marquis remained crouching where they were, not daring to move. Mr. Tregelles and Mademoiselle MontSauvage continued to behave in the same abandoned manner as before, and Charlotte felt herself go hot with embarrassment and indignation. Really! How any gently-bred female could behave in such a way was quite beyond Charlotte's comprehension! And though she knew — at least, she had heard — that men did behave in that manner with — with a certain kind of woman, yet — she could not help being decidedly surprised that Mr. Tregelles should behave so. It really was — was — beyond everything!

Even though he had not exactly said anything, Charlotte had the very distinct impression that the marquis was decidedly annoyed, and she felt that she quite understood his annoyance at Mr. Tregelles' enthusiasm. For still he and Mademoiselle MontSauvage continued in their abandoned way, till long after the sound of the men's footsteps had died away in the distance. The most suggestive scuffles and giggles came from the pair, and Charlotte's embarrassment turned to angry disgust.

It was the marquis who moved first. When all had been silent for several minutes, apart from the pair on the other side of the barn, he rose and strode over to them. Charlotte was at first annoyed that she had been left to get up by herself till she remembered that the marquis thought her a young man, and quickly she rose also, and dusted herself down. She did not hear what the marquis said first, but when she approached them she heard him saying in a very grim voice that they would miss the boat if they did not hurry.

Richard was already on his feet and

pulling on his coat. 'I — I am sorry,' he was apologising, 'Mademoiselle, I can not say sufficiently how much I regret what has happened, but — I could think of nothing else.'

The marquise gave a little gurgling laugh, and Charlotte was sure that she pouted provocatively, and whispered to Mr. Tregelles that she did not think him very gallant. Then she turned to her brother, and told him not to be such a bear.

The marquis only said curtly that they must go at once, took his sister by the arm, and made for the door. Richard Tregelles finished buttoning his coat, and looked about for Charlotte.

'You are all right?' he whispered.

'Yes, I thank you,' Charlotte returned stiffly, ignoring his proffered arm. She followed the marquis and his sister to the doorway.

There was no-one else in the road. The four went outside, and continued through the village as quickly as they could. Luckily, they passed the last of the houses without meeting another soul.

They made better progress along the lane than they had coming up from the coast. Charlotte found it quite impossible to judge the time, and was in an agony that she would hear the clock strike three at any moment. Once or twice Mr. Tregelles put out his hand to help Charlotte when she stumbled over a rough patch, but she ignored him studiously. She was also aware that from time to time Mademoiselle Mont-Sauvage turned round to Richard to suggest that he should walk on the other side of her, and Charlotte, ostentatiously, looked away. But Mr. Tregelles did not move from her own side.

It was when they had left the village well behind them that Charlotte became conscious of a pattering behind them. She glanced back, and saw the shadow of a hound a few yards from them, and knew that the companion of her vigil had rejoined her.

145

Richard Tregelles looked back also. 'I thought we had seen the last of the creature!' he whispered.

'I, also,' Charlotte returned in a low voice, forgetting to be stiff.

But somehow, she felt pleased that the dog had reappeared. He had, after all, been an undemanding companion, who had seemed to sense what he should do when he was with her. Charlotte looked round again, and stopped and waited for the animal to catch up with her. When it did, she stroked its head.

'Really, M — Charles! You must not encourage it!' Richard Tregelles said somewhat exasperatedly.

'It is doing no harm!'

'It might give us away!'

'How might it do that? We are not likely to meet anyone now.'

Richard Tregelles made no answer, but Charlotte knew that he was not best pleased. She felt perversely glad for it.

However, her assumption that they would have an easy passage back to the beach now that they had left the village was a premature one. Certainly they had not far to go: they had left the lane from the village, and were now making their way across fields to the cliff, when suddenly — a soldier with a musket materialised before them!

All four stopped as one and stared appalled. Charlotte heard a low growl come from behind.

'And where might you be goin'?' Charlotte understood him to demand, his musket held ready to fire.

What the marquis replied, Charlotte did not understand, but it was clear that the man was not satisfied. Further words were exchanged between the marquis and his sister and the man, and Richard whispered to Charlotte that the man was suspicious, and was ordering them to return to the village with him.

'I am going to make a run for it, M — Charles,' he went on swiftly; 'I am sure the man will discharge his weapon, and then our friend may tackle him for he will be virtually unarmed then . . . '

'But you may be hit!' Charlotte whispered, greatly frightened.

'It is not likely that he will aim well enough in the dark. But once his musket is discharged, it will take him several seconds to re-load it, and he may be overpowered then.'

But Richard had hardly finished whispering to Charlotte, when a shape hurtled straight for the man's throat. The man was taken completely unawares, and tried to hold the dog off with his musket, but the weight of the animal bore him to the ground. The cries of the man were muffled as the dog's teeth snapped savagely at his throat, and for a second Charlotte buried her face in her hands.

'Come on, run!' Richard urged.

'But — !'

'No buts! Your friend has saved us, and I take back all I said. But we are so late now that we may well miss the boat, and it is also more than likely that this fellow is not alone!'

And without more ado, he grabbed

hold of Charlotte's arm and pulled her after him. The marquis and his sister were already speeding ahead.

Charlotte heard the man still struggling with the dog, and though she was grateful for the intervention, she could not but shudder to think what damage the dog's teeth might inflict.

Suddenly they were at the edge of the cliff above the sea. Unerringly the marquis led them forward till they came to the path down to the beach below them up which they had toiled it seemed so many aeons ago.

As they started to scramble down, there were shouts behind them.

'Your friend has not finished the man off, then!' Richard remarked grimly, as he held Charlotte's arm tightly, and pulled her down far faster than she wanted to go.

'You mean — ?' she gasped.

'I mean that clearly the dog did not savage that man enough!' Richard returned. 'Hurry!'

It was a crazy descent to the sand

below. Slipping and slithering, held upright only by the strength of Richard Tregelles' arm, somehow Charlotte descended the cliff.

As they reached the bottom they could hear shouting above them, and the sound of the pursuers close behind them. Anxiously they pelted down the beach, Charlotte straining her eyes to see a boat standing off shore; but perspiration now dripped from her forehead and into her eyes, and she could barely see a couple of yards ahead.

She thought that her lungs would burst as she pounded over the sand and shingle to the water's edge. But to her unutterable relief, she made out the shape of a small boat, and heard Tregarth's harsh whisper, 'Another two minutes an' us'd 'ave weighed anchor, sir!'

'I know,' Richard panted. 'But as you can hear, we have had some trouble.'

'Us've been stowed an' waitin' this 'alf 'our an' more,' Tregarth went on, as

150

Richard almost lifted Charlotte into the rowing-boat. 'The men've been gettin' restive.'

'We are very grateful indeed, Tregarth,' Richard returned as he scrambled into the boat.

Tregarth pushed the little craft into the water and jumped in after it was afloat. He scrambled to take the oars at once, and with strong strokes began to pull away from the shore. The sound of the following men showed them to be close to the bottom of the cliff.

Tregarth had not taken more than two strokes when there was the sound of splashing in the water beside the boat. Charlotte was sitting opposite the marquis and his sister, and beside Richard Tregelles. Suddenly a huge weight dripping water surged out of the sea and landed beside her, rocking the little craft so that it nearly overturned. All the three men swore, but Charlotte gazed for a moment at the dog's face which was so close to her own. This time she did not try to escape the long pink tongue as it began to lick her face, but she flung her arms round the animal's neck, and began to laugh, hiding her face in the furry neck.

'Let me take one of the oars, Tregarth,' Richard cried urgently as pounding footsteps were heard racing down the sand.

In a moment, the two men were pulling together, and the boat was moving away from the shore, steady again.

The first soldiers reached the water's edge and splashed into the water after them, and then flashes could be seen, and the sound of something heavy dropping into the water with sharp little plops. Charlotte gazed past the dog's head. Already they were several yards from land, and the foremost soldiers, up to their waists in sea-water, were rapidly growing smaller, being now but dim shapes on the shore. Charlotte breathed a sigh of relief that they were safely out of France.

Mademoiselle MontSauvage patted

the dog's head. 'You have a fine animal, Monsieur,' she said.

'I can not think what we are to do with the creature,' the marquis remarked impatiently. 'We shall have to put it into the sea and let it swim back to land.'

'Oh, no!' Charlotte cried appalled. 'I mean — Oh, no!' she repeated, in what she hoped was a more manly tone.

'What are you saying, *mon frère*?' the marquise demanded. 'After all, the creature has saved us!'

The marquis shrugged, and Charlotte clasped her arms more firmly about the dog's neck, determined not to let it go.

'Monsieur Richard,' the marquise said, 'you would not have the poor creature thrown into the sea — perhaps to drown!'

'It does not depend on me, ma'am, but upon Tregarth here,' Richard panted, still pulling on the oar.

'You will let the dog on your ship, will not you, sir?' the French girl asked now, smiling at the smuggler.

Tregarth only grunted for answer. The marquise smiled at Charlotte. 'Do not worry, Monsieur, I will make sure your dog is safe.'

Great as was the dislike that Charlotte had unaccountably taken to the French girl, she could not but be grateful now, and she murmured that the marquise was very kind.

'And how, sister, do you suppose we are to get the dog into the boat?' the marquis demanded now. 'We have to climb up a rope, and I am certainly not going to carry the animal up it!'

'No — o?' His sister returned. 'Well, I tell you this, if that dog does not go with us, then I do not go up the rope either!'

The marquis let out a flood of French then, which was far too fast for Charlotte to understand, but it was cut short by Richard. 'I will carry the animal up myself,' he panted. 'This is no time to play games, Mademoiselle; our friends have waited for us as long as they dared. We must not hold them up longer still.'

'Ah, you are so brave, Monsieur Richard!' the marquise purred.

'May — may the dog not stay in the boat when it is pulled aboard?' Charlotte asked quietly.

It was Tregarth who answered. 'We are not taking the boat aboard, sir. The current will carry it round the point, and our French friends will be able to find it again tomorrow.'

The bigger vessel was standing farther off shore than it had done in Melyn Cove, and all the while they were being rowed out, the occasional shout from those on shore could be heard across the water. But the wind was behind them, and blew stiffly, and in barely a quarter of an hour, they were beside the boat that was to carry them back to England.

With a quick, 'I depend upon you, Monsieur Richard!' the marquise was first up the rope ladder. The marquis went next, and Charlotte watched him somewhat indignantly until she remembered that she was still a young man in his eyes. The dog stood beside her, panting, and she turned impulsively to Richard.

'Can you really carry him, sir?' she asked quietly.

'I promise you he will come,' was the reply.

Charlotte turned and made her way up the ladder as quickly as she could.

Tregarth came after her and at once gave some order to one of his men standing by. The next moment, Charlotte saw something like a sling thrown down to the little rowing boat. As she leaned over the rail, Charlotte could dimly see Richard fix the band about the dog, and in a moment, he gave a quiet call, and the dog was heaved into the air. In another moment, it was on the deck beside Charlotte. One of the smugglers took off the sling, and then Charlotte bent down to hug the animal.

She looked up as Richard Tregelles came onto the deck himself.

'Thank you, sir. I — I could not have borne it if — if the animal had been — thrown overboard!'

'It is certainly not the way to treat a friend,' Richard agreed with a smile.

6

Charlotte remained on deck till the
boat was under way. Her heart lifted as
the sails filled, and the timbers creaked
and the voyage home began. Then
Richard guided her down to the cabin,
and the dog went with her.

The marquise and her brother were
chattering as Charlotte entered the
cabin. The girl stopped as Charlotte
appeared, and came over and stroked
the dog's head.

'I am so glad your dog is safe,
Monsieur.'

'It is not really *my* dog. He — he has
just attached himself to me.'

Suddenly the girl stopped her stroking and looked at the animal keenly.
Then she bent down and smoothed her
hand over the creature's flank. 'You
have seen this, Monsieur?'

Charlotte bent down to see what the

French girl meant. Across the dog's flank and stomach were scabs from long abrasions. The animal turned and licked her face.

'It looks as if the dog has been hit,' the marquise said.

Charlotte caressed the dog's head again. 'Well, it is not going to be hit any more, Mademoiselle!' she vowed.

Richard Tregelles came towards the girls. The dog looked at him suspiciously. 'Perhaps Mademoiselle would care to take the sleeping cabin,' he suggested. 'It is late, but you may have a few hours' sleep before we reach England.'

'Oh, *non, merci, Monsieur*,' the marquise returned, 'I am not at all tired. But — perhaps my brother . . . ' The girl turned to the marquis. 'Do you take it, *mon frère*; we know that you are no sailor.'

In spite of the success of the expedition, the marquis was looking anything but pleased. 'Thank you, but I am quite well,' he returned now shortly.

'I shall remain here with you.'

Sudden fatigue now overwhelmed Charlotte. *She* would be very glad to use the sleeping-cabin if nobody else wanted it; but of course, that was not possible. She was thankful when the marquise sat down, and then Charlotte herself was able to sink into a chair, the dog beside her

Dimly she heard the others talking. She was aware too of the creaking timbers of the ship, and of its rolling when they were out of the lee of the coast and in the open water of the Channel. But luckily, this time the regular motion did not disturb her. Indeed, she felt very well, except for an overwhelming tiredness.

She must have fallen asleep sitting in the chair, for when next she opened her eyes, the marquise and Richard Tregelles were seated alone at the table. The marquise's hand was resting on Richard's arm, and she was looking at the Englishman with an expression that made Charlotte almost blush to see it.

The ensuing conversation only confirmed her opinion that the marquise was what Charlotte's mother would have called a pert little baggage.

'I think you liked it — very well,' she said with a giggle.

'Mademoiselle,' Richard Tregelles replied in a tone which Charlotte was at a loss to understand, 'we were — in a tight spot.'

'A tight spot? What is that?'

'I mean that we were in great danger of capture.'

'Oh, that!' The marquise shrugged. 'But — we are not in any danger now.'

'And therefore I must not take advantage of you again,' Mr. Tregelles answered smoothly.

'Oh, Monsieur Richard! Do not you see that — ' The marquise stopped and smiled, and Charlotte saw then how strikingly lovely was the young girl's face. Surely Richard Tregelles could not be blamed for being bewitched by this entrancingly beautiful creature.

That, at least, was Charlotte's first

thought as she sat quietly in the shadows, watching with fascination. Her second thought was of shocked indignation that such a young girl should so obviously be throwing herself at Richard's head. Really! Charlotte felt exceedingly indignant. After all, this time, Mr. Tregelles could not be said to be encouraging her, and Charlotte had no doubt that her first impression of the young French woman had been quite right! She was a — a shameless hussy!

Charlotte could not but stare as the young girl gazed up into Richard's face, her pink lips parted, her bosom against his arm. The English girl had no wish to watch: indeed, she would have given a good deal to be safely away from persons indulging in such *shocking* behaviour, when suddenly the boat gave a sudden lurch as a sharp gust caught it, and with a thump, Charlotte found herself ignominiously on the floor.

'Oh!' Charlotte rubbed herself, then scrambled to her feet as she saw that the marquise was laughing.

Richard, meanwhile, had jumped up, and came over to her. 'Are you all right — Radley?'

'Yes, I thank you!'

'You are sure?'

Charlotte nodded, rubbing an elbow now.

'Monsieur is tired,' the marquise said with an amused smile.

' — Er — Radley has had a tiring day,' Richard Tregelles said. 'Coming unexpectedly . . .'

'I should thank you, Monsieur,' the marquise now said winningly, 'for all that you have done for me. And, being so tired, why do not you share the sleeping cabin with my brother? There is plenty of room there. If you could support his groans, that is . . . ?'

'Oh, no! I am very well here!' Charlotte cried, taken aback.

'I do not think your brother would care to be disturbed!' Richard Tregelles said equally quickly.

'No, indeed! I would not dream of

'— of —' Charlotte found herself quite unable to complete the sentence, so agitated did she feel at the thought of what the marquise suggested.

'I am sure my brother would not mind,' the marquise said, clearly more amused than ever.

'Really — I — I am quite awake now,' Charlotte declared, rubbing her elbow vigorously. 'Indeed, I am quite hungry!'

'I will see if Tregarth can provide us with something,' Richard returned.

'Oh, no! It does not matter . . .'

'Certainly it does. I will go and ask.' And Richard strode purposefully from the cabin.

Charlotte continued to rub herself.

'Pray, do sit down, Monsieur,' the marquise said, gesturing at the chair Richard had been using.

'Mr. Tregelles will be back shortly,' Charlotte answered somewhat ungraciously.

The marquise smiled. 'Your name is Charles Radley, I think?'

'Yes.' The answer was decidedly brusque.

'You are very brave — to come to France to help rescue me. I thank you for it.'

Charlotte managed to execute some sort of bow, but made no answer.

'I suppose you think I should have come before with my brother?'

Charlotte shrugged, and made some sort of mumbling reply about the marquise having reasons for remaining behind.

'Ah, you have been told, I see — '

'I have been told nothing!' Charlotte said tartly.

Now the marquise rose, and came to Charlotte and placed her hand lightly on Charlotte's arm. The marquise smiled up at Charlotte provocatively. 'Can not we be friends, Monsieur Charles?'

Charlotte jumped back a pace, more agitated than ever. It seemed that the marquise was intent upon flirting with *her* now!

'There is no need to be frightened of me, Monsieur!' the marquise purred, fluttering her long lashes.

'I am not in the least frightened of you, Mademoiselle!' Charlotte gasped, not thinking at all of how her voice must sound.

'No — o?' Now the young girl stepped forward again, and her face was only inches away from Charlotte's own. Indeed, her lips were pursed, almost — almost as if she expected — a *kiss*!

'No!' Charlotte squeaked, retreating again. In doing so, she trod on the sleeping dog's tail.

It jumped up with a yelp, and looked at her reproachfully. Charlotte bent down and made much of it, terrified that the marquise would come yet closer.

But now the French girl burst out laughing. 'Oh! Monsieur! Or — Mademoiselle! Or — perhaps — even Madame! Oh, I thought so from the first — from the way you walked! But — I could not understand how you should be in France! I could not think that the good Richard would permit you to enter such danger. He is much too chivalrous for that, is not he, Mademoiselle?'

'Mademoiselle!' Charlotte repeated, stupefied and alarmed, gazing up at the young face alight with mischief.

'You must forgive me! It is then — Madame?'

Charlotte shook her head, quite bereft of speech.

'Mademoiselle, then. And when I suggested that you should share the cabin with my brother — ! Oh, then I *knew* I was right! If you could have seen your face, Mademoiselle!' And the marquise laughed again.

'Indeed!' Charlotte said shortly.

'Does my brother know?'

'I do not think so.'

'Ah! Only the good Richard. You are his *maîtresse*, then, and he could not bear to leave you behind?'

'Certainly not!' Charlotte cried, hugely affronted, and scarcely able to believe her ears.

'Not! But then — '

'Oh! I have never heard of such a thing!' Charlotte stormed now, her voice suddenly coming back to her, and her indignation flooding forth. She glared at the young French girl. 'You may behave so in France, Mademoiselle, but in England, young ladies of good family do not!'

'No? Oh, how very dull! But — I can not believe it!'

'It is quite true, I assure you!'

Richard's voice now said from the doorway, 'What is it that is true?'

Charlotte turned to look at him, blushing with embarrassment, but also very thankful to see him. She could not utter a word.

Mademoiselle MontSauvage had no such difficulty. 'Mademoiselle has been assuring me that young ladies of good family in England are very — *comme il faut*. I say that it is a pity. It makes for a very dull life!' And the eyelashes were fluttered again, and the hips

168

moved provocatively.

Charlotte thought savagely that perhaps the marquise was afflicted so that she was unable to do other than flirt.

Richard was replying, 'Ah! I see that you have discovered that — '

'But of course,' the young girl replied almost impatiently. 'I see from the first that Mademoiselle does not walk like a man. I do not guess right away, of course; I just think it odd. But now — when Mademoiselle speaks — and I look close to — then I see.'

'We hope that you will keep the secret, Mademoiselle,' Richard now said very earnestly.

'If you wish.' The marquise shrugged. 'But, I tell you, Mademoiselle, in France, young ladies of good family do not dress so.'

Charlotte blushed.

Richard said hastily, 'Nor in England, I assure you, Mademoiselle. It was only that Mademoiselle Radley came to help — '

'Oh, I know! I know! And I am truly

grateful!' And the marquise came up to Charlotte and kissed her affectionately.

Charlotte stood like a statue, but when the French girl stepped back, she found herself smiling into the beautiful face.

'We can be friends, Mademoiselle?' the marquise smiled.

At that moment, the dog took a pace towards the French girl, and looked up at her, wagging his tail.

Charlotte remembered how the marquise had helped ensure that the dog was not tipped into the sea and left to swim to shore as best it could. 'Of course, Mademoiselle,' she returned, and to her own surprise, and in spite of her disapproval of the marquise's shocking behaviour, she meant it.

'Well, now,' Richard went on, 'Tregarth has on board only brown bread and cheese. He is sending some in directly.'

'I shall be glad to have anything, sir,' Charlotte said very sincerely.

★   ★   ★

It was dawn when the English coast was sighted. At first there was only a dark shape dimly discerned in the pale lightening of the eastern sky, but suddenly a red sun jumped above the horizon, the wind seemed to freshen and the sails were filled, the boat appeared to skim through the water, and what had been an amorphous shape took on the outline of cliffs and fields.

Charlotte and the marquise and Richard had come up on deck to walk about a little, and never had Charlotte seen a more welcome sight than the Cornish coast which lay ahead of them. The journey had gone so well that Charlotte even began to hope that what Richard had said would come true — namely that she might be back at the St. Bride's vicarage in time for breakfast.

For the first time she began to think seriously of what might happen when

171

she returned there. Her aunt Radley would undoubtedly be very angry indeed, and might even send her back to Shropshire if the secret of her overnight absence were known. And Kitty — she would be most dreadfully worried, even if she had managed to contain herself and had said nothing. Charlotte gazed ahead, willing the land to come nearer faster.

All at once there came a shout from the man in the crow's nest. Charlotte did not catch what was said, but directly all was bustle on the boat.

'What is it? What is happening?' she cried.

But Richard had already gone to Tregarth to find out what was wrong.

He was back in a few minutes. 'They have had a signal. The Revenue men are waiting at Melyn Cove, I collect. We will have to land somewhere else.'

'The Revenue men! How do they know this?'

'There is a cottage near the coast

172

with a witch's eye. They were warned — '

'A witch's eye! What is that?'

'It is a small round window which looks out to sea. If those watching on shore know that the Revenue men are waiting at the appointed landing place, they put a light in this window to warn the boat to go elsewhere. The look-out spied the light.'

'Where shall we go then?'

'I am not certain. We may have to go round the coast as far as Kynance. But somewhere farther to the south.'

'Is it much farther than Melyn?' Charlotte had visions of her breakfast at the vicarage disappearing at speed.

'I am afraid so. But — perhaps we need not go much farther.'

'What will happen if we are caught?'

'There will be a fight.'

'A fight!' Charlotte repeated faintly.

'You must not worry.' Richard Tregelles tried to sound reassuring. 'Luckily there is a strong wind. We are crowding on canvas now, and we may well get to land without being seen. We received the warning in good time.'

In the growing light, Charlotte watched in trepidation as the sailors hurried about the deck. She saw that the angle at which they were approaching the coast was changing, and instead of making straight for the coast, they were now sailing more to the left. But the boat was cutting through the water more speedily than ever, and even as she peered fearfully behind them, terrified that she would see one of the narrow, swift Revenue cutters at their stern, she began to hope that all might yet be well.

They sped along in this fashion for some minutes, then the man aloft gave another shout.

'We have been spotted, I think!' Richard exclaimed.

Charlotte looked back towards the golden, dawning sky. Sure enough, although it was, as yet, only a speck in the distance, she could make out the lines of another craft racing after them.

'Oh! Do you think we will get away?'

'Tregarth and his men will certainly try!'

The marquise clapped her hands. 'Oh, I had never thought that there would be such excitement in England! I have always thought it such a dull country! But this is — *magnifique*!'

'Not so magnificent for these men if they are caught!' Richard returned drily.

'What have they on board, then? Brandy?'

Richard nodded.

The marquise shrugged once more. 'Ah well, if we are caught — we shall just have to make sure that they do not find it.'

'And how would you propose to do that, Mademoiselle?'

'Oh,' the girl returned airily; 'we shall see.'

And the marquise turned to watch the pursuing boat.

To Charlotte's anxious eyes, it

seemed to be considerably nearer them now. Their own boat was skimming through the water, but the Revenue cutter seemed almost to possess wings, so swiftly did it move. Even as she watched, the gap decreased appreciably. She glanced at Richard Tregelles, and saw that he looked uneasy, if not worried.

He caught Charlotte's glance. 'You need not fear for yourself,' he whispered. 'We are quite safe whatever happens — unless they sink us, that is — '

'Sink us!'

'Oh! I do not really think that it will come to that! But — I feel a responsibility for these fellows. Had it not been for them, we should not have got our friends out of France, and had it not been for us, they would have been away from the French coast earlier, and might well have reached safety before it grew light.'

'But — they have been paid, have not they?'

'Yes. But — it will be our fault if they are caught.'

'Could not you explain?'

'Of course, I shall try. But — I cannot but fear that it will do little good.'

They turned to watch the Revenue boat again. It was much closer now.

'How is it that they are gaining on us so easily?' Charlotte asked. 'We seem to be moving so swiftly.'

'The Revenue boats are built only for speed. Look at her lines. And she has no cargo. She sits much lighter in the water.'

It was then that Charlotte thought she heard a voice calling from the other vessel. 'Heave to, in the name of the King!'

'Did you hear that?'

But their boat continued as fleet as ever, speeding over the waves.

The cry from behind came again.

Now as Charlotte looked, she could actually see the figures on the deck of the following cutter: she could make out the man hailing them.

The men in their own vessel bent grimly to their task of keeping it going at top speed, but the other craft continued to gain on them. Then it was level with them and overtaking them. The call to heave to came yet again.

There was no response, and then there was silence for a short space, as the two boats raced side by side, barely twenty yards apart. The sails were taut as the wind filled them, and the water dashed past the bows with high-pitched flurry.

Once more came the call to heave to, now with the added threat of fire in the event of non-compliance.

Charlotte heard this and was appalled. 'Would they really shoot at us!' she demanded fearfully.

'I am afraid so,' Richard answered grimly.

There was little time to doubt it. Charlotte could see the small cannon on the Revenue cutter trained on them. She watched with fascinated horror as it was made ready, saw a flash, heard an explosion, and then a splash on the far side of their own craft.

'That was only a warning,' Richard Tregelles muttered tautly. 'Next time they'll aim at our mainmast.'

The next moment, Charlotte saw Tregarth uncovering a cannon on their own deck.

Richard saw him at the same time, and cried out, 'Don't be a fool, man!'

'Us'll not be took wi'out a fight, sir!' Tregarth returned.

'You'll salvage at least your lives and your boat!' Richard returned. 'I hired you. Let me talk to them!'

'What can you say, sir? Them knows where us've been!'

'At least let me try!'

Tregarth looked at Richard doubtfully, then shouted some orders. After a moment, the sails began to rattle down the masts, and the speed dropped almost at once.

'These men are soldiers?' the marquise demanded. She had been

179

watching events, obviously excited.

'Revenue men. Customs men,' Richard returned.

'They think to catch the smugglers?'

'Yes!'

'I will speak to them.'

The young girl glanced across at the other boat which was now coming alongside, and abruptly hurried away.

But Charlotte was hardly aware of this as their own craft lost way and was soon still. The Revenue cutter came alongside, and the rope ladder was thrown down.

Charlotte waited in trepidation for the men from the customs boat to clamber onto their deck. A moment later she was gazing in astonishment as Captain Bidder's head appeared.

He looked about him, then his gaze lighted on Richard Tregelles.

'Good Lord, Dick! What the devil are you doing aboard?'

★ ★ ★

After the initial astonishment, Captain Bidder soon resumed his official manner. He was followed by three of his men, all of them armed. They spread across the deck, covering all hands. Tregarth and his men watched them sullenly.

'Well, Tregelles, you'd better explain!' Captain Biddee said bluntly.

'Nothing easier!' Richard replied airily. And swiftly he explained about bringing the marquise from France. 'I hired Tregarth and his boat,' he said, a small grin touching his lips. 'He knows the French coast well!'

'No doubt!' Captain Bidder returned drily.

Charlotte herself kept as much as possible out of the captain's line of sight. She was terrified that he would recognise her.

'You thought also to do a little business on the side, if I mistake not, Tregarth?' the captain went on.

The smuggler only scowled and made no reply, and Richard hastily reaffirmed that he had hired Tregarth and his boat and his crew.

But suddenly an imperious young voice was heard. 'What 'as 'appened? Why 'ave we stopped?' And the marquise swept across the deck, looking distraught. 'Monsieur Tregelles, 'oo are these people? You promised me we would sail as fast as possible!'

'Mademoiselle, allow me to present Captain Bidder. Bidder, this is Mademoiselle La Marquise de MontSauvage, whom we have just succeeding in rescuing from the guillotine. Had it not been for Tregarth and his men . . . well, you may easily guess what might have happened.'

Captain Bidder bowed, clearly much struck by the young woman. Charlotte had never had the least doubt that she was an exceedingly beautiful creature, but now, if it were possible, the marquise looked more lovely than ever. Charlotte saw with astonishment that tears were pouring down her cheeks, but that they caused not the least blotchiness to the perfect skin, nor the least redness to the ravishing eyes.

The marquise went up to Captain Bidder, put both her hands on his arm, and looked at him piteously. 'You 'ave come to 'elp us, Monsieur? Oh, I do thank you! My poor brother! I am so worried for 'im!'

Charlotte saw plainly that it was quite beyond Captain Bidder not to be responsive to this appeal.

'Well — er — not exactly, ma'am,' he began. Then stopped, and added in a concerned voice, 'What — er — is the matter with your brother, ma'am?'

'Oh, I do not know! I am so worried. 'E must 'ave a medicine at once. 'E lie so still. They shot 'im — as we were in the little boat fleeing from our enemies — and if 'e does not see a surgeon soon . . .'

And the marquise dissolved in tears and practically flung herself on the gallant captain's breast.

'I — er — I am indeed sorry to hear that, ma'am, but — it is my duty — '

The captain made a brave attempt.

'Oh, Monsieur! I beg you! Let us go on at once. While we are 'ere, perhaps my brother 'e die in this 'orrid boat! You come! You see 'im!' And the marquise proceeded to attempt to pull Captain Bidder towards the cabin.

'Really, ma'am — '

But the captain had no chance. Even some of the smugglers had stopped scowling.

The marquise continued to haul at Captain Bidder's arm. 'Oh, Monsieur, I do not know what to do, I am so worried . . . '

'I — I am very sorry to hear it, ma'am,' Captain Bidder said awkwardly, 'but I have my work . . . '

'And you do your work, Monsieur, only do let us proceed, I beg you! Oh! If only we could get a surgeon quickly! What shall I do — in exile — if my brother is not 'ere to protect me! Oh, you English are so kind! I know you will 'elp me!'

And the marquise stopped to gaze

imploringly into the captain's face.

'Very well, ma'am, I will come to see the marquis.'

Now, he strode forward, the marquise running at his heels, wringing her hands.

What happened in the cabin, Charlotte did not know, for the captain and the marquise were alone there, but for the ailing marquis. But in a few minutes the pair reappeared; Captain Bidder gave orders for one of his men to remain on the boat, and he himself and his other inspectors returned to their own craft, ordering Tregarth to make for Pentallack, the nearest harbour village, and promising to rouse the local surgeon himself.

In short order they were under way again, making for the sheltered cove. Charlotte, Richard and the marquise repaired to the cabin, the former two anxious to know exactly what had taken place.

The marquise was jubilant. 'There!' she exclaimed. 'Is not that good! The gallant *capitaine* has gone, and we may go to land without trouble.'

'There is still one of his men on board.'

'Oh, pouf! We may push him over! A little slip — !'

'Mademoiselle!' Richard sounded scandalised.

But the French girl laughed. 'Oh, Monsieur Richard! You are so serious. But — what I think is — I will talk to this man, and then, when he is not looking, the brandy may be thrown overboard.'

'I do not think that Tregarth and his men would agree to lose their cargo so easily!'

The marquise shrugged. 'They are fools, then. But — I do not think they need lose it. They can mark it — as they always do. And I will talk to this man while it is done.'

Richard went off to talk to Tregarth about these proposals, and Charlotte was left alone with the French girl.

'Your brother — the marquis — he

was not really hit, was he?' she whispered.

The marquise gave a gurgling laugh. 'Oh, *mon Dieu, non*! My brother 'as only the *mal-de-mer*! Look! I show you!'

'Oh, no!' Charlotte drew back. 'But — I could not but wonder what injury you showed Captain Bidder.'

The marquise laughed again, and thrust her hand into a pocket in her skirt. She brought out a small flat round pot, and held it up for Charlotte's inspection.

'What is that?'

'Oh, Mademoiselle! You English! It is for the *maquillage*. The — the rouge. Under a bandage it looks quite like blood. And when I came down before, I put a bandage round my brother's shoulder.'

Charlotte stared at the younger girl, and suddenly burst out laughing. 'Oh, Mademoiselle! I have never known anyone like you! But — do you really use rouge?'

187

'When it is necessary,' the French girl shrugged. 'Always I have some with me.'

Richard came back then, and reported that Tregarth was willing to try the marquise's plan.

'But we shall have to be quick, for we shall be round Pentallack Point shortly, and in view of the harbour, and the Revenue cutter again.'

Charlotte was the last to go up on deck. The coast was much closer now, and the boat was running parallel with it. She saw the marquise go up to the customs' officer who had been left on board, link her arm through his, and gradually draw him right up to the prow of the boat. Meanwhile, from the stern, barrels were hastily unloaded, which, Charlotte saw, sank at once. How they were marked, she could not see, but she supposed the water, so close in to the coast, could not be very deep.

Charlotte watched anxiously as this went forward, dividing her attention between the marquise and the man at one end of the boat, and the disposal of the brandy barrels at the other. She was in a fever that the man would turn round and see what was being done, but he did not do so once, and Charlotte gave full credit to the marquise for everything. And by the time they rounded Pentallack Point and came into the little harbour, there was not one jot of evidence left to show what the smugglers had been about on their own account.

As soon as the boat was tied up at the quay, Captain Bidder came on board with several customs' officers, and the surgeon. The marquise went down with the medical man to her brother, and very shortly the marquis was brought up, lying on a table top, and was taken off the boat and put into the surgeon's carriage. The marquise went with him.

Richard looked at Charlotte and grinned. 'That is a remarkable young woman,' he said.

'Indeed she is!' Charlotte replied with

great admiration.

It was nearly nine o'clock when they had sailed into harbour. Now Richard went to the nearest inn and easily procured a chaise in which to drive Charlotte to St. Bride's Charlotte, meanwhile, began to worry about what would happen when she returned there. There would be just enough time for her to arrive in time for breakfast, she knew, and there was a chance that this escapade might escape the knowledge of her aunt Radley. But there was no certainty of it, and by the time Richard Tregelles returned with the conveyance, Charlotte had thought herself into a fine state of agitation.

When she came to leave the boat, the dog, of course, was at her heels. Charlotte had scarcely thought of it for some time, but now its presence seemed only to increase the troubles she would face back at St. Bride's vicarage, for it was extremely unlikely that her aunt Radley would take kindly to the presence of the animal in her

190

spick-and-span domain.

'Would you like me to keep the animal for you, Miss Charlotte?' Mr. Tregelles asked.

'I hardly like to wish him upon you,' Charlotte answered doubtfully.

'It would be a pleasure, ma'am.'

'Then, I accept your offer, sir!' Charlotte cried gratefully. 'It will certainly be one less matter for me to worry over!'

She became increasingly agitated the nearer they came to St. Bride's.

'Would you like me to explain to Miss Radley . . . ?' Mr. Tregelles suggested.

'Oh, no! That would be above all things terrible! I mean,' Charlotte went on, blushing, 'I fear my aunt would only imagine — I mean — '

'I understand you perfectly, ma'am.' Mr. Tregelles came to her rescue. 'But — perhaps you may yet enter the vicarage unseen . . . '

'I can not depend upon it greatly, sir.'

But when they reached the village,

there was still some ten minutes to ten o'clock, and Mr. Tregelles had the chaise stopped outside the garden gate, and after a careful survey, Charlotte decided that she must attempt to scale the ivy again. She slipped from the vehicle, and was through the gate and across the lawn in a trice.

But she had forgotten the dog. Just as she reached the ivy, and was about to take her first step upwards, there came the sound of furious barking behind her, and Charlotte turned in consternation to be confronted by the sight of the animal leaping the gate to follow her.

'Hush! Good dog!' Charlotte commanded in a whisper.

Richard Tregelles was out of the chaise in a flash, passed through the gate and across the lawn and grabbed hold of the dog, which promptly began to growl.

'Hush! Oh, do hush!' Charlotte whispered; 'Oh! What shall I do?'

'You leave the creature to me, Miss Charlotte!' Richard said bravely. 'Do you climb up the ivy!'

'But if he should bark again!'

'Pray leave him to me, ma'am. Do you hurry!'

Without further ado, Charlotte began to scale the ivy, praying she had not been seen by anyone in the vicarage. The window was open, and she managed to scramble inside, then turned to see what had become of the dog. She was in time to see Mr. Tregelles, coatless, lifting the dog into the chaise. His coat was over the dog's head, the sleeves wound round the animal's neck. The creature was a mass of struggling body and legs.

The chaise door was slammed upon the two, and started off as Charlotte leaned from the window. She watched as the chaise moved out of sight, then quickly took off her cousin's garments, and donned her own morning gown. There was but little water left in the jug, and she could only wipe her face; she had just begun to comb her hair when the bell for breakfast prayers sounded, and swiftly tying her hair in a ribbon, Charlotte fled from the room and down the stairs.

She entered the dining-room just as her uncle was opening the big Bible. She ran to her chair opposite Kitty, and clasped her hands and closed her eyes, deliberately avoiding her aunt Radley's outraged look.

She felt Kitty staring at her, and wished her chair was beside Kitty's so that she might ask if her absence had been discovered. But she kept her own head down dutifully, and only looked at Kitty when the Bible reading and the prayers were ended. Her cousin was still looking amazed, but gave Charlotte an encouraging smile as she took her seat.

'You were late, Charlotte!' Aunt Radley said in a fearsome voice.

'I am very sorry, ma'am!' Charlotte murmured with a chastened look.

'Did you not sleep well?' her aunt demanded in an acid voice.

'I — am afraid that I did not,

ma'am!' Charlotte replied, all too honestly.

'Hmph!' was Miss Radley's reply, and she turned to her brother-in-law.

By which Charlotte gathered that her overnight absence had not been remarked by her formidable aunt.

Charlotte was very conscious of Kitty giving her questioning looks, and endeavoured to smile meaningly in return, but she felt far too sleepy to spend energy on much else besides attempting to keep her eyelids raised. Even eating, after the first few mouthfuls, proved too much of an effort, and Miss Radley said very tartly that it seemed as if Charlotte were sickening for something, and that she would administer some brimstone and treacle at the conclusion of the meal.

Charlotte heard her aunt say that Tom's leg was mending well, but that the boy seemed to be fretting, but she could not get out of him what was the matter. The girl realised that of course he wanted to know the outcome of her errand. She thought that she must go to him after breakfast.

That thought was the last thing Charlotte remembered before she nodded off completely, and gradually her head came to rest upon the table itself, amidst the breakfast dishes. Of Miss Radley's scandalised cries, and Kitty's concerned questions and Anne and the younger boys' giggles she was completely oblivious, lost in a deep dreamless sleep.

7

Somehow Charlotte was got upstairs and into bed without really waking. In the face of such a genuine malady Miss Radley grew concerned, and allowed the girl to sleep as long as she could, sensibly believing that such was the best remedy for indisposition. By the time dinner was served that day, Charlotte was restored to her usual good spirits and sprightliness, and the cause of her sleepiness remained a secret to all but Kitty and Tom.

When she came downstairs for the meal, she learnt that the marquis and Mr. Tregelles had called earlier in the day with the marquis's sister, recently come into England from France; and that they had all been much disappointed not to see Miss Charlotte.

'But M. MontSauvage said that he

would come again tomorrow, Charlotte, and oh! he was so melancholy that you were not with us!' Kitty said with shining eyes. 'I really do believe — oh, Charlotte, I am quite certain that he likes you exceedingly!'

'Are you, Kitty?' Charlotte's voice was strangely vague.

'Charlotte! I thought that — well, I was sure that you had a *tendre* for M. MontSauvage! Why, I am sure you told me so! Only a few days ago!'

'Yes,' Charlotte answered somewhat doubtfully. 'It is true, Kitty, that I do find him quite the most agreeable young man whom I have ever met.' Charlotte finished robustly, almost as if convincing herself.

'Perhaps when he comes tomorrow, Charlotte — he will ask for you!' Kitty said excitedly. 'Now that his sister is safe — and how very beautiful she is! — he may be able to think of such things!'

'Oh! Do you think so, Kitty?' Charlotte cried, feeling unexpected alarm. 'I mean — I do not really think — '

'Charlotte! Charlotte! what has happened to you? Do you no longer *like* M. MontSauvage?'

'Oh, yes, I — I like him very well!'

But to Charlotte's own astonishment, she was aware suddenly that there was something different in her feelings for the handsome Frenchman. Quite what, she was not sure. But perhaps, when she saw him again, her previous emotions would be restored.

★ ★ ★

The marquis duly turned up at the St. Bride's vicarage the following morning. This time he came alone. Charlotte and Kitty were sewing in the morning room — items for their aunt Radley's poor basket — when he arrived, and to Kitty's excitement and Charlotte's consternation he was not shown in at once, but was heard to enter the vicar's study.

'Oh, Charlotte!' Kitty breathed, eyes shining.

Charlotte affected not to understand her cousin.

'But why else should M. MontSauvage see my father alone?' Kitty demanded reasonably.

'There might be any one of several reasons to account for it!'

But Kitty shook her head, and would believe nothing but that the marquis was come to ask permission to speak to Charlotte.

Miss Radley was soon heard to repair to her brother's study, and some little time later she came to the morning-room, and ordered Kitty to go with her.

'I need your help with the new sheets,' she said by way of explanation.

'I will come and help you also, ma'am!' Charlotte cried, jumping to her feet.

'Indeed you will not, Miss!' her aunt retorted instantly. 'You will please to remain here!'

And with no further word of

explanation, Charlotte found herself alone.

But she had barely time to attempt to regain command of herself when the door opened again, and her uncle came in with M. MontSauvage.

'Ah, Charlotte, my dear, there you are,' her uncle said brightly.

Charlotte curtseyed to the marquis, who smiled and bowed in quite the old way.

'You have heard my great news, Mademoiselle?' he demanded, coming up to her. 'My sister is safe in England at last, and — *I* am able now to — to think of my own affairs!' And he gave her a melting smile.

'I was indeed delighted, sir, to hear that your sister is now with you,' Charlotte answered, blushing a little under the intensity of his gaze.

'My sister was desolated not to see you yesterday,' the marquis continued. 'But I hope very shortly to have the pleasure of presenting her to you, Mademoiselle.'

'I, too, shall look forward to making Mademoiselle's acquaintance,' Charlotte murmured, acutely conscious of the lie she was uttering. She allowed herself to gaze squarely at the marquis. Surely he must suspect something! But no! His smiling look was quite unconscious.

'A most delightful child,' the vicar beamed. 'So unfortunate that you were indisposed yesterday, my dear. But now, my dear niece, I collect that M. MontSauvage wishes to speak with you. He has spoken with me first, as I am, at the moment, standing in the place of your dear father, and — I have seen no reason to deny his request. I am sure, my dear, that there is no need for me to ask you to hear our guest out.'

And still beaming, the vicar removed himself from the room and closed the door upon them.

For the first time, the marquis looked at a little less than his usual ease. Charlotte, although outwardly composed, was inwardly anything but calm.

Kitty had clearly been quite right, and indeed, had not M. MontSauvage hinted that he would speak to her as soon as his sister was safe? She should be flattered that he had lost so little time, and after all, was not this what she had wanted — ever since she had first met him? Was he not so very handsome and distinguished? A man of such sensibility and culture? What more could any woman possibly want?

It was, therefore, disconcerting in the extreme, when Charlotte discovered that she would really prefer M. MontSauvage to say nothing at all.

However, it was far too late to withdraw now. She would just have to manage as best she could.

The marquis took some steps towards her, apparently with the intention of catching hold of her hand.

Charlotte backed away to a sofa, and sat down, at the same time indicating a seat at a little distance from her own. 'Pray will you not be seated, sir?' she said with as much composure as she could muster.

The marquis put his hand to his heart. 'Oh, Miss Radley — Miss Charlotte! I could not be seated at this moment! My feelings are too much for me! I hardly know how to compose myself!' And he gazed at her with intently smouldering eyes.

'Is — is there anything amiss, sir?' Charlotte asked, it being obvious that the marquis expected her to say something.

'Mademoiselle! Nothing is amiss! And everything is amiss!' the marquis said dramatically.

'Oh, sir. I do not under — '

The marquis came yet closer. 'I could not speak before, Mademoiselle. You know how I was worried for my sister. But — now that she is safe — I — Mademoiselle — I am able to consider my own happiness!'

Swiftly now the marquis crossed the few remaining yards between them, flung himself down on his knees beside her, and seized her hand.

Charlotte's heart started racing away — in a fashion not dissimilar to the beam engines she had seen at the mines in the area of St. Bride's. She attempted to withdraw her hand, but the marquis clung fast.

'Oh, Miss Charlotte — ever since I first saw you at Lord Pentallack's ball — you have been to me the epitome of all that I could ever desire in a woman! You must have seen how I have admired you! Beautiful and accomplished as you are, how could I help it? Your hair, your eyes, your fingers — as you play upon the instrument — all are a poem — '

The marquis broke off here, and pressed fervent kisses upon the hand he held.

'Nevaire — nevaire — ' he continued, his words growing increasingly French in pronunciation as his excitement grew, 'nevaire 'ave I met a woman 'oo so enraptures me!'

The marquis kissed Charlotte's hand again.

'Everyt'ing about you, Mademoiselle,' he went on, 'is — perfection personified! You light the room you are in, Mademoiselle, and the other women fade away like the moon does before the sun! I 'ave only to see you, Mademoiselle, you 'ave only to enter ze room, and — my 'eart begins to beat — like a pomping-engine — boum! boum! boum! Ah, Mademoiselle, you must 'ave 'eard 'ow it beats against my ribs! Oh, Mademoiselle! Oh, Charlotte! I love you! I love you! Oh, *mon amour, je t'adore* . . .'

And the marquis promptly began kissing Charlotte's hand again, and then, before she quite knew where he was, his lips had moved up her arm, and he was kissing her elbow, her shoulder, her neck!

It had no sooner dawned on Charlotte what the marquis was about, and she had decided it must cease, when he seized her face between his hands and began kissing her lips!

Charlotte's astonishment was at first

so great that she was capable of no rational action. Her attempt to push the marquis away was purely instinctive. The thought flashed through her mind that at one time this would have been the very peak — the pinnacle of happiness — to have the marquis in the middle of a proposal before her — but now it was happening, she was not at all sure. It was, after all, quite different from how she had thought it would be. Certainly, the marquis was gratifyingly passionate, and he had said a great many things very proper in such a circumstance — not that he had actually asked her to marry him yet, but doubtless that would come — but still, she did wish that he would stop! Really, she could not understand herself at all! It was extraordinary that, with the fascinating M. MontSauvage's arms about her, she felt none of the things she had thought she would feel. Far from being swept away into a delightful vortex of passion, drowning in undreamed-of delights as happened on such occasions in all the best novels — far from that occurring now, she was all too conscious of how — *ridiculous* — the marquis was being.

Not only that, he was pressing her against him so very tightly that the buttons on his coat were sticking into her most uncomfortably.

No. There really was no doubt that she was not swept away at all. And however much she might have thought she wanted this, now that she had it, she really did not want it at all. It came to her very forcibly that she did not want the marquis's arms about her, nor were his kisses such as would carry her into the undreamt fields of felicity . . .

And — in the inkling that she realised this, Charlotte also realised just whose arms she did want about her, and whose protestations of love she did long to hear. Her rational self shouted most inopportunely that having once been mistaken, she might well be mistaken again. But her heart sang out, 'No! I know now! *I know*!'

She attempted again to push the marquis away, more firmly now. But he clung to her all the more tightly.

'My lord! Please!' she managed to get out in a moment when the marquis himself drew breath. 'Pray, let me go, sir!'

The marquis only attempted to kiss her mouth again, but Charlotte, pushing with all her might, managed to turn her head quickly, and the kiss landed on her ear.

'Oh, sir! I must beg you to let me go!'

Her words had no effect whatsoever. The marquis only continued his embrace, murmuring between each kiss, 'Oh, Charlotte, *mon amour*! Exquisite! So modest! So — so — Eeengleesh! *Je t'adore*!'

'But I do not adore you, sir!' Charlotte cried wildly, thinking that she might never escape from this man who had as many arms as an octopus. 'Pray, stop! Stop!' She was aware that she was almost bawling now. Oh, why did her aunt Radley not make an entrance now!

Her words must have impinged at last upon the marquis's consciousness. He withdrew his head a few inches and looked at her with smouldering eyes. 'What is this, *mon amour*?' he demanded, deep in his throat.

Now Charlotte managed to get her hands against the Frenchman's shoulders and pushed hard. 'I am not your love, sir! I am afraid that in that you are quite mistaken!'

'Mistaken! How is this? I can not be mistaken!' And the marquis attempted to kiss her again.

But Charlotte managed to hold him off, though the strain upon her arms was very great. 'Oh, indeed, indeed you are, sir! Quite, quite mistaken!'

The forcefulness of Charlotte's words must have made an impression, for the marquis now looked into her face with incredulity. 'What is it that you say, Mademoiselle?' he blurted out, clearly completely astonished.

'I said,' Charlotte returned slowly

and deliberately, 'that you are mistaken, sir!'

'But — I can not be! You love me, Mademoiselle! You know you do!'

'Indeed I do not, sir!' Charlotte declared with some heat. 'That is what I am trying to tell you. I regret it very much, but you are mistaken in thinking that my liking for you is the affection which is due between husband and wife!'

'Husband and wife!' the marquis almost stuttered. 'What is this of — husband and wife?'

'Were you — were you not asking for my hand in marriage, sir?' Charlotte faltered.

'Indeed I was not, ma'am,' the marquis said with some hauteur. He rose to his feet. 'I am a *marquis de France*, Mademoiselle, and must marry a lady of equal rank. Sixteen quarterings have my family had now for over eight generations. And — sixteen quarterings must my wife have! Oh, no, *mon amour*! I am not talking of

211

marriage. I speak of *love*! *Amour*! The grand passion that a man feels for a woman! That sweeps him off the earth and into the heavens of delicious delight when he is in her arms! Oh, Charlotte, my love! My queen! The only woman whom I could ever — '

'Let me understand you rightly, sir!' Charlotte cried now, astonishment giving way to anger. 'Am I correct in apprehending that you do not speak of marriage, have no intention of marriage, indeed, but that what you suggest is — is — a — dishonourable association?'

'Dishonourable association! Nevaire! To be the true love — the only love — of the Marquis de MontSauvage can never be dishonourable! I do not understand you, ma'am!'

'And I do not understand you, sir! In England, a gentleman does not make such a proposal to a lady!' Charlotte's voice quivered with indignation as she glared at the marquis.

The marquis was clearly taken aback.

'I do not understand! It is a most honourable estate that I offer you! The King himself might take a *Maîtresse en Titre* who would be first after the Queen herself! A second queen, indeed, with far more of power and influence than anyone else in the whole country!' The marquis stood, waving his arms in large circles to describe the power of the French King's *Maîtresse en Titre*.

Charlotte jumped up also. 'But in England that is not so! In England respectable women do not receive such — such Cyprians! In England they are kept in decent seclusion and are not flaunted to the indignity of honest women!'

'Kept in seclusion! *Nom d'un Nom*! I could not see La Pompadour being kept in seclusion! She, who guided the taste of the country for years!'

'All this is to no purpose, sir! I — I accept the fact that you intended no insult, but I have to tell you, sir, that had I a brother, and were he to hear of what you have suggested, he could do nothing less than call you out!'

'Call me out! What is this?'

'Fight you, sir! With pistols or swords as you might choose, but he could do nothing less than attempt to deprive you of your very life!'

The marquis looked more and more amazed. '*Mon Dieu*! What kind of country is this? It is impossible to understand it! In France we have the greatest civilization that the world has ever known. *Le Roi Soleil* brought us to the height of power and glory, and yet — you in England do not do as we do in France!'

'No, sir, we do not! And — I would remind you, sir, that our Duke of Marlborough had something to say to your King Lewis — !'

'Malbrouk!' The marquis's face darkened. 'Ah, yes, Malbrouk! I had forgotten — ' He stared at Charlotte in silence for some moments, then abruptly executed an elaborate bow. 'Excuse me, Mademoiselle,' he said stiffly, and still more stiffly, left the room.

Charlotte stared after him, her breast heaving with indignation. Then abruptly, the funny side of the whole situation struck her, and she began to laugh. It seemed that the power of His Grace of Marlborough was still puissant, for it had taken only the mention of his name to cause the Frenchman to turn tail and depart.

Her peals of laughter rang out, and in another moment, her aunt Radley put her head enquiringly round the door.

'Well, child?' Miss Radley's face was alight with grim curiosity. 'Well, Miss, and what did his lordship have to say?'

She came into the room, followed by Kitty and the vicar. She looked about with baleful enquiry.

'And — where is M. MontSauvage?'

Charlotte was now laughing so much that she had to wipe the tears from her face. The others stared at her in astonishment which quickly turned to consternation.

'My dear!' the vicar murmured; 'you are not well!'

'Oh, indeed, sir!' Charlotte gasped, endeavouring to control her mirth; 'I beg your pardon, but — I am very well!'

'But what has happened, child? Did his lordship speak?' Miss Radley demanded, her voice very terrible.

'Oh, yes, ma'am! He spoke! Indeed he spoke! And to good purpose!'

'And what did you say, child? You accepted him, I suppose?'

'Er — no, ma'am.'

'No!'

Three pairs of eyes regarded her in astonishment.

Charlotte shook her head, and repeated 'No.'

'But — why ever not?' Miss Radley gasped finally. 'Surely you must see that it would be a very great thing to be a marchioness?'

'I suppose it would, ma'am. But — I was not given the opportunity.'

'But — you have just said that the marquis spoke!'

'But he did not offer for my hand, ma'am.'

Miss Radley's jaw dropped at least two inches. 'Did not offer for your hand, Miss?'

'No, ma'am.'

'Then — of what did he speak, Miss?'

Charlotte was seized by the temptation to tell her aunt exactly what it was which the marquis had offered, for the pleasure of seeing her aunt's scandalised expression. But prudently she held her tongue.

'Of — this and that, ma'am.'

'I do not understand you, Miss!'

'My dear,' her uncle now said in his gentle voice, 'what can you mean? When the marquis spoke to me, I had quite the impression that — that — ' His voice faded away.

'Oh, Charlotte, I am so sorry!' Kitty cried, flinging her arms sympathetically round her cousin. 'What a terrible disappointment for you. I made sure — '

'Oh, no, Kitty! It is no disappointment, I assure you!'

'Not!'

'No. Indeed, that is why I was laughing — to think what an escape I have had — '

'Escape!'

Charlotte nodded vigorously. 'Yes! Escape! For I really do not think I could ever be happy with — with a foreigner!'

'But my dear, why should M. MontSauvage ask me so particularly if he might speak to you alone?' the vicar said doubtfully.

Miss Radley seconded her brother's question with a suspicious glare.

'I really can not say, sir,' Charlotte answered as insouciantly as she could. 'Perhaps his lordship changed his mind,' she added brightly, better invention quite failing her.

'But I do not understand . . . ' her uncle pursued, his kind face screwed up with puzzlement.

'No, indeed!' Miss Radley now said

in fearsome tones. 'Changed his mind! After he has been paying you such attentions these last weeks! It is not at all the thing, sir, and you will have to *speak* to him!' And she eyed her brother in a manner that would brook no argument.

'But, my dear — what could I say? I mean, it is quite possible that the marquis fully intends to speak later. And I do not think that he has exactly *trifled* with Charlotte — '

'His attentions, to me at least, appeared extremely marked.'

'Oh, I beg that you will say nothing, sir!' Charlotte cried, her laughter now quite gone before the terrible possibility which her aunt might bring about. 'It is true that I have enjoyed the company of M. MontSauvage, but — that there has been anything serious in it . . . Oh, no! There has been nothing like that!' And she looked from her uncle to her aunt with a good deal of consternation. 'Indeed, as I have already said, I am convinced that I could not be at all happy with a foreigner. I really do like plain, *English* things best!'

'Hmph! I am glad to hear it!' And Aunt Radley eyed her at first suspiciously, and then her face gradually softened to an expression of approval. 'You have more sense than I thought, child! Really, I have rarely seen a man with more ridiculous manners — such a poppycock as he was, prinking about, and forever kissing one's hand! I had thought that being a ladyship had quite turned your head, girl!'

And Miss Radley favoured her niece with a truly benevolent smile.

'Oh, no, ma'am!' Charlotte hastened to assure her. 'I could never be happy with — with such a person at all!'

The vicar ceased to look puzzled, and smiled with relief that he was to escape any unpleasant interview with the Frenchman; but Kitty continued to regard her cousin with uncomprehending commiseration, and when the two girls were alone, Charlotte had to spend a considerable time assuring Kitty that

truly she had suffered *no* disappointment.

But when she was by herself,
Charlotte faced the fact that, even if it
were true that she had not been
disappointed by the marquis, she was,
nevertheless, in an unhappy situation,
recognising as she now did that she was
deeply attached to one by whom she
could have no hope of having her
feelings reciprocated.

* * *

Two whole days went by before
anything was heard from those at
Pentallack, and then Richard Tregelles
and Mademoiselle MontSauvage called
at the vicarage with the news that she
and the marquis were to travel to
London the very next day. The marquis,
it seemed, was in low spirits, and
certain that only the air of the
metropolis would do him any good.

'I am so sorry to miss his lordship,'
Charlotte said composedly, 'But

delighted to make your acquaintance at last, Mademoiselle.'

'And I you, Miss Charlotte,' the French girl said; 'I have heard so much of you.' This was accompanied by a broad grin.

Charlotte wondered if the marquis could have told his sister what had occurred between him and Charlotte. She supposed it was possible, but on the other hand, she could not think that the marquis would be one to confess a failure.

'You intend to live in London, Mademoiselle?' Charlotte continued, thankful that she would not see the marquis again, at least for the time being. His departure meant avoiding a deal of awkwardness.

'There are many of our countrymen there,' the marquise replied, 'and of course, we hope for the success of the Allied arms in soon procuring the downfall of those who now rule France. My brother is anxious to be on hand.'

'And I dare say you have many friends there?'

'Certainly we shall have at least one,' the marquise said, with a warm smile at Richard Tregelles, which cut Charlotte to the heart.

'And it will be a deal more exciting than Cornwall,' Richard added with a smile which Charlotte could barely match. 'You will be the first to appreciate that, Miss Charlotte.'

Charlotte blushed. 'Oh, no! I — I have indeed enjoyed my stay here.'

'You are returning home, ma'am?' This came very quickly.

'Oh, no! I mean — not quite yet. But my stay so far — has been very agreeable.'

It seemed that the young man would say something more, but the marquise now said, 'Monsieur Richard is so kind as to come with us to London. Lord and Lady Pentallack are so kind as to lend us their house there.'

Charlotte could not look at Richard as her heart plummeted to her shoes.

So, he had fallen for the beautiful marquise — as was only to be expected!

'Will you be away long, sir?' Kitty asked, thereby relieving Charlotte of having to make the effort to enquire herself.

'I do not know. Some weeks, perhaps.'

Charlotte had the impression that Mr. Tregelles was regarding her oddly, but as she could not raise her eyes to his, she could not be sure.

'We hope to persuade Monsieur Richard to remain a long time,' the marquise now said. 'After all, I believe that the season will be starting soon . . .'

The dismals settled firmly on Charlotte's shoulders, and it was only with the very greatest effort that she managed to take any further part in the conversation at all.

But when Richard went on to ask for the latest news of Tom, and while Kitty was speaking of her brother, the marquise drew Charlotte a little aside and said in a low voice, 'I feel I have not thanked you properly, Mademoiselle, for all your help. I regret very much that we are to leave so soon that you and I may not become good friends; but — my brother — he is in a very strange mood, and nothing will please him but to go to London at once. For me, I expect to enjoy myself wherever I go, but — I am disappointed not to know you more. Perhaps you will come to London one day, Miss Charlotte?'

'Sometimes my parents take a house there.'

'Then we must certainly meet if you come. I shall depend upon you.'

It was lucky that the marquise's attention was called for then, for Charlotte was not sure that she could have answered the French girl as candidly as her friendly overtures required.

And after the visit of the marquise and Mr. Tregelles, Charlotte was the object of renewed condolences from Kitty, who thought her cousin's gloom was dependent upon the fact that the marquis was to leave the neighbourhood so hastily.

'But, Kitty!' Charlotte declared wearily, 'I have told you that I am not the least interested in M. MontSauvage — at least in that way!'

'But Charlotte — something must have happened when he was with you — to bring this about, I mean! We heard nothing of any departure before this! Are you sure you did not — ?'

'I expect it is really that Mademoiselle MontSauvage would prefer it there,' Charlotte returned dully. 'You know how fond of his sister is the marquis, and he will like to do whatever pleases her.'

'Oh, poor Charlotte! I am so very sorry!'

'There really is no need, Kitty!' Charlotte answered, making an effort to sound cheerful, but beginning to feel irritated by her cousin's insistence upon her having suffered a disappointment.

But of course, Kitty was quite right

to feel sorry for her cousin, though she could not guess the real reason.

* * *

However, a distraction was provided in the next few days by the preparations for Kitty's eighteenth birthday party. There was to be a small dinner-party, and there was to be dancing afterwards, and it cost Charlotte a good deal of effort to be cheerful so as not to cast a blight over her cousin's happy day. She had never before been so overwhelmed by gloom, and really, it was not at all a pleasant feeling.

However, when the birthday itself arrived, an event occurred which no amount of dismals on Charlotte's part could have blighted for Kitty.

Bob Pritchard came to the vicarage early on the birthday morning with a present for his cousin, a pretty gold enamelled box with 'Kitty' inscribed upon the top. Kitty, of course, was highly delighted, and showed it to everyone several times; and on the third occasion that she held it up for her aunt Radley's inspection, Miss Radley, busy with her preparations for that evening, and beginning to grow somewhat fractious through anxiety to see that all was precisely as it should be, said quite sharply,

'Yes, yes, Kitty; it is a very pretty thing. But do take your cousin away. You are forever under my feet, Bob Pritchard, and how you expect me to have everything arranged for this evening . . .'

The three young people, well aware of Miss Radley's tongue, rose hastily and left the room.

'It is a delightful day,' Kitty said, beaming at Bob Pritchard. 'Let us go and get out hats, Charlotte.'

And the two girls went upstairs. Charlotte sighed as she tied the ribbons under her chip hat, and thought how much pleasanter it was when the party from Pentallack had used to come, and she could walk with them, and not have to play the gooseberry.

But when they came downstairs, Bob Pritchard was nowhere to be seen. Puzzled, the two girls went into the garden, but the young man did not seem to be there either.

Kitty was at once upset. 'Surely he — he could not have gone — without saying goodbye!' she murmured with quivering lip.

'Of course not, my love!' Charlotte said firmly, putting her arm about her cousin's shoulders.

The two girls wandered in the shrubbery for some little time, each disconsolate in her own way, but for Kitty the dismals did not last long, for after about twenty minutes, Bob Pritchard suddenly appeared before them, beaming all over his face. Kitty was at once transformed and ran to meet him, asking him where he had been.

It took Charlotte less than a second to see that she was exceedingly *de trop*, in quite a different way from being a mere gooseberry, and tactfully she slipped away and left the two alone.

When next she saw Kitty, her cousin was wearing a delightful ring upon the third finger of her left hand, and Kitty was laughing and weeping and exclaiming that it was quite the best birthday present that she could have received; the remainder of the day passed in a great haze of happiness, and even Charlotte was able to forget her own wretchedness in long stretches of rejoicing in her cousin's felicity.

But in the following days, Kitty's state as a duly-affianced female only served to underline Charlotte's own situation, and never before had she found life so dull and stupid. She attempted to imagine as little as possible what might be happening in London to the party from Pentallack, and it was not merely the loss of schemes for enjoyment which had now ceased, that caused the gloom to descend. Charlotte was in love for the first time, and for the first time also what she wanted was quite out of her power to acquire.

She would have returned into Shropshire, but for the fact that her cousin's wedding was to take place fairly shortly. As there was no longer any need for her to act as chaperone, she was much on her own, and came to spend a good deal of time with her cousin Tom, whose leg was mending well, and who seemed to have acquired a rather more serious and grown-up outlook on life since his accident.

Charlotte did not in the least begrudge Kitty one jot of her happiness; but she did wish that a few crumbs of joy might fall at her own feet.

8

It was nearly two weeks since the marquis had come to St. Bride's vicarage to make his extraordinary proposal, ten days since the party at Pentallack had departed for London, and four days since Kitty had received her father's blessing to her betrothal.

The weather was bright and warm, and one morning Kitty and Bob were walking through the bluebell wood arm in arm, content to be together; while Charlotte was sitting among the gravestones in the churchyard, a quiet retreat where she hoped she not to be disturbed, and where the age-old yews, dark and gloomy, accorded well with her own melancholy feelings. Her cousin's wedding was not to take place for another month, but Charlotte wished yet again that it was to be immediately, so that she might return to Shropshire and home. The summer surfeit of parties and picnics, balls and excursions, would soon take her out of herself, and Charlotte was seriously considering the possibility of writing to her mother to ask her to request her own immediate return home, when her attention was caught by the sound of a twig breaking behind her. Startled, she was just about to turn her head when the dog which had attached itself to her in France came bounding up to her, wagging its tail and smiling all over its doggy face.

At once Charlotte's heart gave a great leap of joy, realising that if the dog were there, then Richard Tregelles must be also; and to cover her confusion which she was occasioned by the involuntary little cry she gave, she stooped down to put her arms about the animal, and after a moment she had collected herself sufficiently to be able to look over the furry back towards the sound of the cracking twig. As she had known she would, she made out the figure of Richard Tregelles standing in the shade of the huge yew trees watching her, having just come through the little gate which connected the vicarage garden with the churchyard. As their eyes met, Richard smiled and came forward into the sunlight.

For a moment, Charlotte's sight was dazzled, and the man's figure seemed to be framed in a golden haze. For a second, Charlotte wondered if she were seeing a mirage, but the dog was warm and solid beneath her fingers, and when Richard spoke, she knew it was no phantom that was before her.

'Charles has not forgotten you, you see, Miss Charlotte,' he smiled.

'Charles?' Charlotte's voice was soft and not quite steady.

'I have called the dog that. I hope you do not mind. He had to have a name.'

'Of course. Why — Charles?'

'After you, Miss Charlotte.'

'Oh!' Charlotte felt herself blush, and rose to her feet. 'You — you have been returned from London long, sir? I had thought — you meant to stay some time there.'

'I returned late last night. Or rather, this morning, ma'am.'

'You — had an agreeable time in London?'

'Always I prefer Cornwall, ma'am.'

'Will you — will you sit down, sir?' Charlotte asked, seating herself again on the table-tomb, and gesturing at one near at hand, for all the world as if she were in a drawing-room. The dog at once put his paws up on her knees, demanding attention.

'I — I have taken great care of Charles for you, ma'am. He did not care for London, though, any more than I did.'

'I am exceedingly grateful to you, sir.'

'It has been — is — a pleasure, ma'am,' Richard smiled. 'But I am sure that he would much prefer to be with you, Miss Charlotte. I think he does not care for men. He barely tolerates me.'

'If you would be so kind as to keep him a little longer, sir — until I return into Shropshire? It should not be for many more weeks. My cousin is to be married within the month. Luckily, there is not need of delay.'

'Ah, yes, Miss Kitty and Bob Pritchard. I am very happy for them.'

'We are all very happy, sir.'

'But — you speak of returning home, ma'am! I — I had hoped that you would stay to see Cornwall in summer. It is particularly beautiful then, when the cliffs are covered with sea-pinks, and the hedges with dog-roses. And — there are a great many other places I should like you to see, Miss Charlotte.'

'I — I have been here near two months, sir.'

'So long, ma'am! It does not seem so long to me.'

Charlotte knew not how to reply, but looked down blushing, stroking the dog's head.

'But then,' Richard went on, and Charlotte could hear the teasing in his voice, 'I recollect that you did find Cornwall — painfully dull.'

'Oh, no, sir! You arranged so many schemes of pleasure — truly I have enjoyed myself here very much!'

'I am so glad that — our excursions have given you pleasure, Miss Charlotte. But,' Richard went on ruefully, 'I dare say you will be very glad to return to your home again. I fear that Cornwall can not hope to compete — '

'Oh, you quite mistake the matter, sir!' Charlotte said quickly. 'Were circumstances such that I — I had to remain here always, I should be most happy — I mean, I do think Cornwall a very beautiful country, sir . . . ' Charlotte's voice faded with embarrassment.

'Would you? Would you indeed, ma'am?' Richard's face was suffused by a brilliant smile.

'Oh, yes, sir!' Still Charlotte could barely look up, as she continued to fondle the dog's head.

'That is — excellent news, ma'am!'

There was a short silence, during which Charlotte endeavoured to think of something to say, while Mr. Tregelles continued to beam at her.

'You have returned to Cornwall — for a particular reason, sir? We had thought you meant to remain in London for the season,' she managed to get out at last.

'I have indeed returned for a particular reason, ma'am!' Richard said very definitely. 'Circumstances suddenly changed. Besides — Charles did not at all care for London.'

'You have not returned — because of a dog!' Charlotte stared astonished.

'Not because of the dog, ma'am — but — but because of the dog's owner.'

'I do not understand you, sir!' Charlotte said faintly, blushing very much.

In a trice, Richard was beside her and had taken hold of her hand.

'Oh, Miss Radley! Charlotte! It was because of you! I returned because of you!'

'Of me, sir!' Charlotte's voice came

out as barely more than a squeak.

'Yes, my dearest love! Because of you!'

'But — the marquise! What of her?'

'What of her indeed? If it had not been for her, I should still be languishing in London — '

Charlotte stared at Richard, almost as wildly as he was staring at her. A huge joy was welling up inside her. 'How do you mean, sir?'

'It was she who told me that you had refused her brother. Oh, I did not realise it at first, but of course that accounted for MontSauvage's wish to depart for London so suddenly — '

'Refuse the marquis!' Charlotte was both affronted and astonished. 'Is that what the marquise said?'

Richard looked into her face fearfully. 'You — you did refuse him?'

'I did indeed!' Charlotte said roundly.

'Oh, my dear love! For one moment, I thought I had been mistaken. And I could not have borne that!'

'Could not you, sir?' Charlotte

whispered very tenderly.

'No, indeed! But, as soon as I heard that, I set out for Cornwall immediately, and could hardly possess my soul in patience till this morning. And now that you have told me that — that in certain circumstances you would not mind at all remaining in Cornwall for the rest of your life — would you — my dearest love — ever consider remaining here in Cornwall with me?'

'How — how do you mean, sir?' Charlotte asked softly, her answer already prepared, but this time, determined to be absolutely certain of what she was being asked before venturing upon a reply, though in her heart of hearts she had no doubts.

Charlotte had stopped stroking Charles's head for some moments now. At this point, the dog jumped up and began pushing his nose against the hand that Richard was holding, whining, and demanding renewed attention.

An expression of irritation crossed the man's face. 'I fear I am doing this very badly, ma'am — and this hound is no help! I do believe he is jealous of me!'

'Oh, surely not!' Charlotte smiled, and pushed Charles away, and sternly, bade him sit.

But for the moment, Richard seemed put off his stride. 'The fact of the matter is, Miss Radley, that — that I have no experience of this sort of thing, and with Charles taking in every word, I confess to feeling somewhat at a loss!'

'Oh, pray do not let him discompose you in the least, sir!' Charlotte cried, suddenly feeling exceedingly elated.

Richard ran one hand through his hair in a gesture of despair. 'Had it been possible, I suppose I ought to have asked advice as to how I should proceed before I began. I dare say MontSauvage had no such difficulty, and in any other circumstances I should have asked him — taken a leaf out of his book — '

'I am very glad that you did nothing of the kind, sir!' Charlotte cried. 'And you have not the least need to consult anyone: least of all M. MontSauvage. A — a quantity of flowery language can sometimes obscure, with very unfortunate results, what should be straightforward and plain. I always prefer simple, unadorned, *manly* English . . . '

Richard stared at her, then carried her hand to his lips and kissed it fervently. 'Oh, Miss Radley! Miss Charlotte! You are an angel!' And he pressed renewed kisses upon Charlotte's fingers.

Charles, not liking the total lack of attention, whined a little.

'Oh, Charlotte, my love! You know what I would say — I really am proceeding very ill — '

'Not at all, sir. You are proceeding excellently.'

'Well, then, my love, here it is: I love you — more than to distraction, and will never be comfortable again if you do not promise to be my wife. And — and if you will not marry me either,

Charlotte, I shall go straight to join His Royal Highness on the Low Countries, and once there I shall do my very best to get myself killed!'

And Richard stopped to draw breath, and gazed at her with rather wild eyes.

Charlotte gazed down into his face, her own alight with love and laughter. 'My dear Mr. Tregelles, there will not be the least need for you to do anything so very drastic! Indeed, should you do so, you would be depriving me of every chance of happiness in this world, which I collect is not your intention, and I, sir, would take it very unkindly!'

'You mean that, my dearest love!'

Charlotte nodded.

'You mean that — you love *me*?'

Charlotte nodded again.

'And not MontSauvage?'

'Not the least little bit!'

The next moment Charlotte found herself most satisfactorily enveloped in Richard's embrace. She would have remained totally lost to every other circumstance of her surroundings but for the fact that after a very few moments, Charles was totally unable to contain himself, and he jumped up and importunately demanded his share of the attentions that were going.

'Wretched creature — !' Richard declared wrathfully.

'Oh, pray do not scold him!' Charlotte begged. 'He is only happy for us!'

'Did ever man have a more difficult time!'

'Difficult, sir!'

'Indeed, yes! Had you ever had to propose, my love, you would know exactly what I mean! What with the unaccustomed difficulties of the thing itself, and not being quite certain of your feelings for MontSauvage, then on top of all that, to have this hound — '

'Not certain of how I felt for M. MontSauvage!' Charlotte exclaimed.

'The marquise may have been mistaken — I did not know . . . And when he was here, you were always with him — '

'I hope that you would not imply that
— that I flirted with him!'

'Of course not, my love! Though
sometimes — it did seem — '

'Oh, how can you, sir!' Charlotte
cried, incensed. 'As if I would after
what he said to me — what he
proposed — !'

Richard Tregelles looked at Charlotte
suspiciously. 'Just what did he propose,
my love?'

Charlotte was conscious of a slip. It
would never do to let Richard know
exactly what the marquis had wanted.
He would certainly feel that he would
have to call him out, and when there
was a duel, one never knew what
might happen. 'To think that you
should think that of me, sir!' she cried
in affronted tones; 'After your behaviour in the barn — with Mademoiselle
MontSauvage . . .'

'That was purely expediency, my
love!'

'It looked to me at the time as if you
were enjoying it very greatly, sir!'

Charlotte retorted with only partly mock-severity.

'Never! Never! It was all that could be thought of at the time!'

'Who thought of it?'

'I confess that — ' Richard stopped abruptly.

'So — it was the marquise herself!' Charlotte said silkily. 'Well, I am not surprised.'

'But — I promise you that it shall never happen again!' Richard declared with a laugh.

'I should hope not, sir! And, though I do not admit for one moment that I was so immodest as to flirt the very least little bit with M. MontSauvage, perhaps we may call it quits. But — did you really think I was attached to M. MontSauvage?'

'When I left here I — I was certain of it. Indeed, I thought that when MontSauvage so suddenly decided to go to London, that you might feel you had been badly used by him. I — I imagined you — unhappy, and longed to stay near you, but could not bear to. Oh, Charlotte, it was only when Mademoiselle MontSauvage told me very positively that you had turned down her brother, that hope sprang again, and I returned here at once . . . '

And at this point, Richard again took Charlotte in his arms, whereupon Charles grew more excited than ever, so that the embrace was interrupted to the dissatisfaction of both humans, and Richard and Charlotte had to be contented with walking about among the gravestones, their arms very closely linked.

'I am afraid that I have made a very bad hand of this,' Richard sighed ruefully. 'I had not thought that I would have to contend with a jealous dog!'

Charlotte laughed happily. 'I would not have had it one whit different, sir!'

'I could have wished it a deal more eloquent and graceful and — and romantic!'

'It could not have been more romantic, sir!' Charlotte whispered.

247

'And I began to despair, my love. When I think how I have loved you — from the moment I first saw you — and now this — '

'Was it really so, my love!' gasped Charlotte.

'Of course it was!' Richard retorted, sounding very shocked. 'From the moment I set eyes on you at my parents' ball, I thought you were quite the most beautiful, charming, delightful, intelligent, fearless, brave, exceptional female I had ever encountered!'

'Did you really think all that, sir!'

'Of course I did! The half of it I could see, and the other half, I knew. After all, I had guessed it was you and Miss Kitty at Melyn Cove that night. Of course I was in love with you at once! And if I had not also at once received the painful certainty that you were already far too interested in MontSauvage, I should have made it known to you a good deal sooner.' And Richard looked at her very reproachfully.

'In love — even then!' gasped Charlotte. 'Oh, my dear love!'

And this time, because Charles had run forward to investigate some matter of keen interest to canine noses, Richard was able to embrace Charlotte in a manner exceedingly satisfactory to them both.

* * *

When Richard went to speak with the vicar who was standing in loco parentis to Charlotte, he found that Mr. Radley accepted the situation with great benevolence and hearty good wishes, and a promise to write to his brother immediately, recommending the match as an excellent one. Miss Radley, when she learned what was on hand, after a few moments' stupefaction, thoroughly approved, and unbent so far as to call Charlotte 'her *dear* child', and was at once full of plans and satisfaction.

'*Much* better to marry an Englishman, dear child! I really could not see what there was to make a fuss about in that young foreigner. Much too pleased with himself, I always thought. Far too fond of seeing what effect he was making — and I do grant that he did make an effect — especially with silly young girls! I had quite thought you were one of them, Charlotte; I am very happy to learn that you have more sense after all!'

Anne clapped her hands, and said that she could not understand why Richard had been so long about it, for she had been certain all along that he was in love with her cousin, and the two younger boys only saw it in terms of yet one more good feed.

It was, to Charlotte's surprise, her cousin Kitty who looked doubtful. She appeared to think that Charlotte had engaged herself upon the rebound, and she much regretted the fascinating marquis.

'But — he was so romantic, Charlotte! So very handsome! So charming — so altogether delightful!'

'So is Richard!'

'Yes, but — '

'No buts at all, Kitty, my love! I am far too happy for that! You must believe that this is quite the best.'

'But I have known Mr. Tregelles all my life! I can not think — '

'You have known your cousin Bob Pritchard all your life — '

'But that is different!'

'Yes, it is!' Charlotte laughed. 'You are in love with him — just as I am in love with Richard!'

And Charlotte's face was so radiant that Kitty had to believe her, and they rejoined the others, the two happiest girls in the kingdom.

Then they all retired to Tom's room to tell him what had happened, and he was delighted with the others, pumping Richard's hand and declaring he couldn't think of a man he would rather have for cousin, and informing Richard that Charlotte was a regular go-er.

'The very best, Dick!' he beamed.

'I know that, young Tom!'

The vicar apologised for not having any good wine to offer in which to drink the newly-betrotheds' health, but produced some excellent brandy.

'Just a little which I have saved since before this war,' he murmured as he poured out the golden liquid.

Miss Radley hurried away to order orange wine for herself and her nieces, and Charlotte and Kitty exchanged laughing glances.

'Perhaps now that Mr. Tregelles is joining the family,' Charlotte ventured with a significant look, 'he might be able to use his influence — with his friends, the gentlemen — to restock your cellar, sir!'

Richard grinned, but disclaimed any such influence, and the vicar murmured hastily that he would not dream of it, but that when this was gone, they would just have to possess their souls — or rather their stomachs — in patience, until this war was over.

And Charlotte was just about to

make some allusion to the cache in the shrubbery when there came a great scuffling at the door, and Charles, whom Miss Radley had forbidden to leave the ground floor, came bounding into the room.

'Really, I have never known such a dog!' Richard cried. 'It is forever quite shamelessly playing gooseberry!'

'Oh, he will get used to it all in time,' Charlotte laughed, stroking the silky head. 'I know!' she exclaimed, 'we must find a companion for him also!'

★ ★ ★

Later that day, when Charlotte and Richard had been most tactfully left alone, except for the omnipresent Charles, and Charlotte's head was nestled most contentedly upon Richard's shoulder, thinking that there was really nothing so agreeable in the world, Richard suddenly said,

'By the way, Miss Radley, a small thing I have omitted to mention . . .'

'And what is that, sir?' Charlotte asked dreamily.

'Now that we are betrothed, for so I consider us, although your father has yet to send us his consent, I shall not agree to your going off upon any more adventures! They are a great deal too dangerous, and I shall not like to have the anxiety — knowing you as I do, — and your propensity for dressing in entirely unsuitable garments . . . '

Charlotte looked up into Richard's face, laughing. 'I do not think,' she said softly, 'that I shall want to go off on adventures any more. For I think now that I am embarking upon the greatest adventure of all!'

THE END

We do hope that you have enjoyed reading this large print book.

Did you know that all of our titles are available for purchase?

We publish a wide range of high quality large print books including:
Romances, Mysteries, Classics
General Fiction
Non Fiction and Westerns

Special interest titles available in large print are:
The Little Oxford Dictionary
Music Book, Song Book
Hymn Book, Service Book

Also available from us courtesy of Oxford University Press:
Young Readers' Dictionary
(large print edition)
Young Readers' Thesaurus
(large print edition)

For further information or a free brochure, please contact us at:
Ulverscroft Large Print Books Ltd.,
The Green, Bradgate Road, Anstey,
Leicester, LE7 7FU, England.
Tel: (00 44) 0116 236 4325
Fax: (00 44) 0116 234 0205

CONVALESCENT HEART

Lynne Collins

They called Romily the Snow Queen, but once she had been all fire and passion, kindled into loving by a man's kiss and sure it would last a lifetime. She still believed it would, for her. It had lasted only a few months for the man who had stormed into her heart. After Greg, how could she trust any man again? So was it likely that surgeon Jake Conway could pierce the icy armour that the lovely ward sister had wrapped about her emotions?

TOO MANY LOVES

Juliet Gray

Justin Caldwell, a famous personality of stage and screen, was blessed with good looks and charm that few women could resist. Stacy was a newcomer to England and she was not impressed by the handsome stranger; she thought him arrogant, ill-mannered and detestable. By the time that Justin desired to begin again on a new footing it was much too late to redeem himself in her eyes, for there had been too many loves in his life.

MYSTERY AT MELBECK

Gillian Kaye

Meg Bowering goes to Melbeck House in the Yorkshire Dales to nurse the rich, elderly Mrs Peacock. She likes her patient and is immediately attracted to Mrs Peacock's nephew and heir, Geoffrey, who farms nearby. But Geoffrey is a gambling man and Meg could never have foreseen the dreadful chain of events which follow. Throughout her ordeal, she is helped by the local vicar, Andrew Sheratt, and she soon discovers where her heart really lies.